## Praise for Margaret Daley

"Decoy suspects lead to an unexpected conclusion—
and a solid and captivating story."
—*RT Book Reviews* on *The Baby Rescue*

"Crisp dialogue combines with abundant action and
mystery."
—*RT Book Reviews* on *Standoff at Christmas*

"Action and intrigue start early on and will have the
reader rooting...for justice to prevail."
—*RT Book Reviews* on *Guarding the Witness*

## Praise for Susan Sleeman

"Sleeman's writing captivates the reader from the
first page in this briskly paced tome. Exciting details
combine to create unpredictable and memorable
scenes."
—*RT Book Reviews* on *Emergency Response*

"Fast-paced action and suspense abounds."
—*RT Book Reviews* on *No Way Out*

"The mystery will keep you involved until the end."
—*RT Book Reviews* on *The Christmas Witness*

**Margaret Daley**, an award-winning author of ninety books (five million sold worldwide), has been married for over forty years and is a firm believer in romance and love. When she isn't traveling, she's writing love stories, often with a suspense thread, and corralling her three cats, who think they rule her household. To find out more about Margaret, visit her website at margaretdaley.com.

**Susan Sleeman** is a bestselling author of inspirational and clean-read romantic suspense books and mysteries. She received an RT Reviewers' Choice Best Book Award for *Thread of Suspicion*, *No Way Out* and *The Christmas Witness* were finalists for the Daphne du Maurier Award for Excellence. She's had the pleasure of living in nine states and currently lives in Oregon. To learn more about Susan, visit her website at susansleeman.com.

# HER BABY'S PROTECTOR

## MARGARET DALEY
## SUSAN SLEEMAN

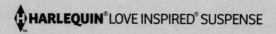

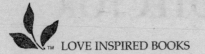

LOVE INSPIRED BOOKS

Recycling programs for this product may not exist in your area.

ISBN-13: 978-0-373-45693-2

Her Baby's Protector

Copyright © 2017 by Harlequin Books S.A.

The publisher acknowledges the copyright holders of the individual works as follows:

Saved by the Lawman
Copyright © 2017 by Margaret Daley

Saved by the SEAL
Copyright © 2017 by Susan Sleeman

# CONTENTS

# SAVED BY THE LAWMAN

## Margaret Daley

To my husband, Mike.
Thank you for forty-six wonderful years.

Yea, though I walk through the valley of the shadow of death, I will fear no evil: for You are with me; Your rod and Your staff, they comfort me.
—*Psalms* 23:4

# ONE

Kate Forster lunged to the right then the left, loosening her muscles before her run. "Are you ready, Jamie?" She bent down and looked under the canopy on the three-wheel, jogging stroller.

Her fifteen-month-old son grinned. "Go, Mama."

"Okay, hang on tight." Kate gripped the handle and started down her favorite route in the large park.

In the Remington Nature Reserve, the path took her through the woods and along the lake. The beautiful dose of God's beauty renewed her after a long day as an Oklahoma family court judge, trying to figure out what was the best decision for the parents and children who ended up before her.

She needed the reminder the Lord was in control, especially after the day she'd had. She hated having to take a child away from a parent, but in this case she'd had no other choice. Not when a little girl's life was in danger. The wails from the mother still rang in her mind.

Kate shook the memory from her mind and focused on her son giggling and urging her with, "Fatter. Fatter." His word for faster.

Kate nodded at a couple who passed her going the opposite way. She often saw them here.

The breeze from the south cooled her as she headed into the wooded part of the reserve. The sounds of birds chirping blended with Jamie's laughter. Both wonderful to hear.

A large man with jet-black hair—another frequent runner at Remington—overtook her and went around them, giving her a smile and a nod. His gleaming gray eyes stood out against his tan complexion and dark hair. She'd seen him a couple of times at the courthouse too. Was he an attorney?

As she rounded a curve in the path, she slowed. A tree trunk had fallen across the trail, probably from the thunderstorm and high winds last night. She'd need to lift the stroller over it if she wanted to continue. She came to a stop and decided to let Jamie out of the stroller while she hoisted it over the downed tree. She still felt wound up after her stressful day.

She picked her son up, his dark brown eyes—the same color as hers—widening.

He began to wiggle. "Down."

Maybe she would let him play a little here then run back toward her car. She stood him on the path then eased down onto a lower branch of the tree trunk. The second she sat, exhaustion invaded her body. "You can play for a few minutes then we'll head back."

"No back."

Her mistake was to stop and take a seat. "Sorry, honey, but it's been a long day. Mommy is tired."

"Me not." He picked up a stick and poked it into the ground. It broke. He looked up at her, a pout tugging at his mouth.

She heard the scrunch of footsteps coming from the other side of the tree trunk. As she rose, she turned to see who it was. Her gaze zeroed in on a thin man about six and a half feet tall, wearing a ski mask—definitely not what someone would have on in April while exercising. When he saw that she'd spotted him, he leaped off the ground and vaulted over the log at the same time Kate whirled and raced toward her son a few feet away.

She scooped Jamie up in her arms as the man landed less than a yard from them. Her gaze connected with his dark one. She shivered at the piercing stare. He grabbed for her son, grasping his legs.

A scream erupted from Kate as the assailant tugged Jamie toward him. His scent of sweat and cigarettes nauseated her, making her want to get away from him. But she couldn't let go. Her toddler wailed while clinging to her. She kicked out and connected with the kidnapper's leg. He stumbled back, letting go of Jamie's legs.

"Help, help! Someone's taking my baby," she yelled as she clutched Jamie against her chest and scrambled as fast as she could backward.

Her son's cries reverberated through her mind. Her attacker stalked toward her, reaching for Jamie again. Caught between the kidnapper and the fallen tree's trunk, she spun to the side, shielding her child with her body as she tried to clamber over the wooden barrier.

The accoster clasped her shoulder, his fingers digging into her flesh while he yanked her back.

Another scream came from the depth of her being. Did anyone hear it? Would anyone come to help?

Detective Chase Walker lengthened his strides as he chewed up the distance to Remington's lake. He'd spent all day hunting down a burglar, finally catching him and then interrogating him, and now he relished the feel of the fresh air and the pounding of his feet against the earth.

Peace. Calm. Two things he longed to have that always seemed just out of reach. After fighting in the Middle East, all he wanted to do was put those memories behind him. But each night they haunted his dreams. For three years.

A scream pierced the air.

He halted.

A cry for help followed.

He spun around and raced in the direction of the sound, going around a long curve in the trail.

Judge Forster, whom he'd passed earlier, struggled with a tall man on the other side of the fallen tree. Chase pumped his legs as fast as he could, closing the distance between them.

The assailant in a ski mask glanced at Chase, then tried to wrestle something from the judge. She held on tight.

Was it her child?

The attacker backed away, stumbled over the stroller and went down.

Chase sailed over the downed log as the tall man scrabbled to his feet and took off.

Chase's right foot hit the ground first then the left, that leg nearly crumbling under him at the impact. He shoved away thoughts of the throbbing ache. "Okay, Judge Forster?" Slowing, he swung his attention to her on the ground by the tree, as she cuddled a crying child.

"We're fine. Get him," she said in a tight voice.

Chase increased his speed, the attacker at least a football-field length ahead of him. The leg he'd wounded as a US Marine overseas continued to protest. Each time he struck his left foot against the hard packed ground, needles of white-hot pain seared him. Nearing one of the small parking lots, Chase had to slow to half speed. But when he heard a car starting, he dug deep for one last burst of energy.

He came into view of the row of vehicles. At the other end he glimpsed a white sedan leaving. Too far away to catch, especially with his SUV in another parking lot, but at least he got the license plate number.

He dug his cell phone out of his pocket and started back toward the judge and her child. He speed-dialed the police station and reported the attack. The sergeant would put out a BOLO on the car. Chase told the sergeant he would take down what happened from Judge Forster.

By the time he returned, she was standing by the stroller, cradling her child against her chest and swinging him gently as she hummed a soft tune. She glanced at him briefly, her brown eyes so dark they were almost black. Once she'd noticed it was him, not her attacker, she focused on her son, dressed in blue shorts and shirt. He was still whimpering a little, but his cries had softened.

Chase waited. He had two brothers and one sister, all younger than him. While growing up, he'd babysat many times and knew when it was important to remain quiet. While he waited, he assessed the judge, who was trying to calm her child. Her long blond ponytail swished as she rocked her son. His gaze skimmed down her length and noted a couple of scratches on her legs, probably from a tree branch. Other than that, she seemed uninjured. And her expression showed that her earlier fear had faded but not the tension that pulsated from her, shouting that she would protect her child at all costs. Their gazes connected for a few seconds. He'd never met her, but he knew who she was. Her reputation as a judge was stellar—fair and compassionate but tough when needed.

He looked away to take in the crime scene. The tree trunk hadn't been there yesterday when he'd jogged this path. Had the assailant set this up? It had looked like he was trying to take the judge's child. A foiled kidnapping or something else?

After the judge placed her now sleeping son in the stroller, she walked toward him. "Did he get away?"

Chase nodded, noting she was about a foot shorter than her attacker. Impressive that she'd managed to fend him off until he'd arrived. "I'm Detective Chase Walker with the Cimarron City Police Department. I got the car's license plate number and called the station. That information has gone out to the officers on duty. There's a chance one of them will spot him before he ditches the vehicle."

"Undoubtedly, it was stolen."

Probably. But not always. "Tell me what happened. I'm going to record this since I don't have anything to write on. Start with your name." Chase punched the record button on his cell phone.

She looked back at her son, then rubbed her temple and said, "I'm Kate Forster. Oh, you already know that." She grinned but couldn't maintain it. "I had my son, Jamie, with me in his stroller while I went for a run. It happened so fast. I'll do my best to tell you everything, but can we do it at my house? It'll be dark soon, and frankly I don't want to be here when it is." She rubbed her hands up and down her arms.

"That's fine with me. I'll take some photos then we can leave. Which lot are you parked in?"

"The second one."

"That's where mine is. I'll follow you back to your house."

"I appreciate it. I've seen you at the courthouse. I thought you might be an attorney."

He started snapping pictures. "Nope. Just testifying in court."

"Can you show me your badge?"

"Yes, it's in my car." He smiled. "I'm glad you asked. You can't be too careful."

"Sadly, I've discovered that in my job, and today only emphasized it."

So had he—both as a Marine and a police officer.

When they left, the judge pushed her stroller, gripping the handle so tight her knuckles whitened. "I've never felt unsafe here. I come to the reserve a lot. This is one of Jamie's favorite places."

"If you're going to continue coming here, don't come alone."

She slanted a look at him, flipping her ponytail over her shoulder. "You don't have to warn me. I might have to content myself with swimming in my pool instead."

"Where do you live?"

She gave him her address.

"That's a nice area of town. Isn't that a gated community?"

She nodded and stopped at a blue luxury car. "Maybe until I open my pool, I'll jog in my neighborhood. We have private security that patrols."

"Or find someone to go with you besides your child. My SUV is in the next row. I'll get my badge and be right back."

As he made his way to his vehicle, he favored his leg. Each step flooded his mind with thoughts of his last time in battle. He still didn't understand how he'd survived when everyone else on the recon mission had died. He should have died, but he hadn't.

Kate pulled into her garage and carefully lifted Jamie out of his car seat. He was still asleep. She stared down at his peaceful face looking so much like her deceased husband, James, even down to the cleft in his chin. The only thing of hers in him was the shape and color of his eyes.

When her husband died in a plane crash while flying

to Dallas, her life had fallen apart. Then in the midst of mourning, she'd discovered she was pregnant again and weeks further along than any of her earlier, unsuccessful pregnancies. Somehow she managed to pull herself together for Jamie, but today when she thought she might lose him, too, that feeling of devastation had swamped her momentarily. She'd hung on to Jamie in a tug-of-war with her attacker. Had he been after her or Jamie? Maybe he'd intended to hold her child for ransom? Her husband had left her a wealthy woman.

"Is everything okay?" Detective Walker's deep, baritone voice cut into her musings.

She blinked and centered her attention on the man who had saved her and Jamie. "Just trying to figure out why that guy attacked me. Let's go inside. I'll have Rachel put Jamie to sleep."

"Who is Rachel?"

"My live-in nanny. She has been a lifesaver this past year."

"How long has she worked for you?"

"Since Jamie was born fifteen months ago. She came highly recommended, with a great résumé. If you're thinking she had anything to do with what happened at the reserve, you can stop. She didn't." Rachel was more like a little sister than an employee. Kate headed for the door into the utility room.

"Do you have a dog?"

When she entered the home, her big white cat was waiting for her. "No. I only have Boss."

He chuckled. "I'm not sure I want to know why you call your cat Boss."

"Because he thinks he runs my house. It's easier letting him think that than fighting with him all the time." He was ten years old and a present from her husband.

"So you don't have a watchdog?"

"No, but I have a state-of-the-art alarm system."

"A guard dog is one of the best protections."

"Do you have one?" Kate lifted Jamie out of the stroller.

"Yes. But no place is one hundred percent safe."

"That's not very comforting."

"I say that to stress the importance of vigilance."

Could she have avoided the confrontation at the reserve if she had been more in tune with her surroundings? The jogger had nearly been at the downed tree before she'd heard and acknowledged his presence in her mind.

Rachel entered the kitchen, took a look at Kate and asked, "What's wrong?" then fixed her gaze on Chase Walker.

"Detective Walker stopped a man from attacking me."

Rachel moved across the room. "Are you and Jamie okay?" She peeked at the child, his head lying against Kate's shoulder.

"Yes. He wore himself out. Please put him to bed while I talk with the detective."

Rachel took Jamie from her. Her son's eyes fluttered open but then closed again when he saw his nanny.

While Rachel left the kitchen, Kate walked to the cabinet. "Do you want something to drink? Water? Iced tea?"

"Actually, water sounds great after jogging."

"I agree."

Kate fixed two glasses, handed him one and then made her way into the hallway. "Let's talk in the den."

She lived in this room filled with photos, books and comfortable furniture. In the corner was Jamie's toy box, which he usually made a beeline for every time he came into the den. Kate settled onto the overstuffed maroon-and-navy couch while the police detective took the chair across from her, giving her a good view of him, all six feet.

His short black hair, damp with sweat, lay at odd angles. But what drew her was his silver-gray gaze, alert, intense.

Earlier she'd noticed he was favoring his left leg. "Did you hurt yourself running after the attacker?"

He kneaded his thigh. "Not really. I was injured three years ago, and occasionally it'll flare up when I push myself."

"I'm sorry you had to do that for me. No doubt you were off duty."

"A police officer is never totally off duty. There's something in our makeup. We can't ignore a person in trouble."

"And for that, I'm grateful." She reclined back and relaxed for the first time since the attack. There was something about Chase Walker's presence that was reassuring. She looked into his eyes and felt safe. "What do you need to know?"

He fished out his phone again, setting it to record. "Tell me what happened."

Kate relived the incident, replaying it in her mind as she went through what she remembered, parts of the attack already foggy. Her heartbeat sped as words tumbled from her.

"What do you think he was after?"

"I don't know. Other than my wedding ring, I wasn't wearing or carrying anything of value."

"Did he say anything to you?"

"No. He cursed when I kicked him. I wasn't going down without a fight."

"Do you think it was a kidnapping attempt?"

She wanted to say no but couldn't. "Possibly. Or he was coming after me, but I was holding Jamie. Maybe he wanted to get Jamie out of the way? It is hard to say."

"Any gut feelings?"

"Do you believe in those?" The intensity pouring off

of him further soothed her fear. At this moment no one would hurt her or Jamie.

"Yes. A couple have saved my life in the past. We take in nonverbal cues, sometimes not even realizing it, and process what they mean. That's where a gut feeling comes from. At least that's what I think. So any hunches?"

She closed her eyes and reviewed again what she remembered in her mind. "Yes. I think this was personal. Why was the tree down over the path I usually use when I come to the reserve?"

"So a planned attack. Okay. Do you follow the same schedule every day?"

"Am I predictable?" She drew in a deep breath and thought about her routine. Usually, she got up every morning, spent some time with Jamie before she headed for the courthouse. She often had lunch in her office while she worked so she could spend more time with her son later. She frequently left for the day by four unless a court session ran longer. "Yes, especially during the weekdays. When I come home, I either jog for half an hour or longer, depending on how Jamie is. He likes to run with me. If the weather is bad, then I stay home and put music on and dance. My son loves to do that, too."

"But if the weather permits, you run outside during the work week?"

"Yes. I'm indoors all day at the courthouse. My cases can get intense. Exercising helps relieve my stress."

"That's why I run, too."

Her deceased husband would only swim, sometimes even in cool weather. He'd been talking about enclosing the pool in the backyard right before his death. Her world had ended that day, too. Her son had saved her from the abyss of sorrow she'd wallowed in right after James had died.

"So Rachel is your live-in nanny."

It wasn't a question, but she said, "Yes. I was going to stay home longer than six months after my son was born, but the person who was filling in while I was on maternity leave quit suddenly. Rachel was already working for me part-time, freeing me up for a few hours every day to run errands and get things done. When I needed her to switch to full-time, she was available to step right in, allowing me to get back to work. In the long run that had been a good decision."

"Is there anyone who might have a grudge against you?" His gray eyes, the color of a thunderstorm brewing, locked with hers. "Who do you think would do this?"

Before she could answer, the detective's cell phone rang.

He looked at the caller's name. "Sorry. I need to take this." He punched his answer button and put the phone to his ear. "Has the car been found?" Chase listened for a moment then disconnected.

"Do you have a lead on the attacker?"

He rose, slipping his cell phone into his pocket. "Yes, the car belongs to Zed Hammer. Do you know him?"

The name of a father who had threatened to make her pay last month for her judgment against him in court chilled her deep into her bones. Was the attack motivated by revenge?

# TWO

The color drained from Kate's face. She sat forward and crossed her arms over her chest. "Yes. Is Zed Hammer my attacker?" Her voice quavered as she said his name.

"He owns the vehicle the man used to escape."

"Has the car been found?"

"No. We haven't been able to locate Mr. Hammer, either."

Kate shot to her feet, her arms stiff at her sides. She balled her hands so tightly her knuckles whitened. "So he could try to kidnap my son again. He told me when the trial was over that I would regret my decision to only permit him supervised visitation with his children." She closed her eyes for a few seconds and shuddered. "The look he gave me told me he meant every word he said."

Her gaze flitted from the two windows in the den to the door as though she expected the man to rush into the room. When she hurried into the hallway, Chase followed her to the foyer where she set the alarm, checked that the front door was locked then hurried to the kitchen and did the same with the doors to the garage and the backyard. When she'd finished doing that, she spun toward him. "What else can I do to make sure Jamie is safe?"

She held herself so rigid he was afraid she would snap.

He covered the distance between them and took a trembling hand, searching for a way to reassure her.

"I'll stay as long as you need. Do you have any family nearby?"

"No. Both James and I were only children. His mother and father live in Australia, while my mother is widowed, too, and lives with my grandmother in Florida. She takes care of Nana, which is a full-time job. I don't want her to even know about what's going on. She has enough to deal with. I don't want her worrying about Jamie and me."

Chase drew her toward the nearest chair at the kitchen table. After she was seated, he sat next to her. "The police are looking for Zed Hammer. With his car being used in the attempted kidnapping and now that I know about his threat against you last month, I'm sure we'll get a warrant to search his house." He would call the station about Kate's connection to Hammer. He wanted to be out there seeing to the details of the search, but at the moment he would be best utilized staying near Kate. She was right to be concerned the man might return and try again. "Tell me what he looks like." Chase wanted to keep the conversation going to distract her from running every scenario of what could happen through her mind.

Kate stared at her lap for a long moment. "He could be the attacker. Mr. Hammer is about the same height and build. I think his eyes were dark like the man at the reserve, but I'm not sure. Oh, and he had a little girl about my son's age."

"Did you notice a white compact car following you anytime lately?"

"Seriously? White is the most common color for a vehicle, so in the last month I'm sure some have driven near me. But I don't remember seeing the same car behind me for long." She dropped her head and rubbed her hands together. "I've never really thought about the traffic around me unless there was a problem. Coming home from work, I'm usually decompressing. I don't like bringing my problems home. I love my job, but it can be emotionally draining at times. I don't want my child affected by that."

"I know what you mean. I don't have a family but if I did, I would feel the same way. Being a detective is challenging and rewarding when I can solve a crime, but I've seen things I wouldn't want to share with my loved ones." Not just as a detective but as a Marine, fighting in a war zone. Memories he'd tried to avoid leaked back into his thoughts. The sounds of gunfire all around him. The stench of death in the air. The agonizing pain streaking up his leg. The fight to keep that injured limb.

Rachel appeared in the entrance. "Jamie is asleep. I won't be surprised if he slept until morning. Do you want me to put in one of the casseroles you made this weekend?"

"That would be fine. I need to change out of my jogging clothes. I'm going to check on Jamie, too." Kate rose.

"And I'm going to check your house and make sure it's secured." Chase shoved his chair back and stood, trying to shake that last skirmish from his mind.

But as he left the kitchen with Kate, the memory stayed with him. He'd been the only one from his team who had survived. So many of his combat buddies had families. He hadn't, but he'd lived while they'd died. That had challenged his faith through the months of recovery stateside.

"There are five bedrooms upstairs," Kate said as she mounted the stairs.

"I'll start there. Are your windows wired to your security system?"

"Yes."

"That's good."

"That room at the end of the hall—" Kate pointed to the left "—is Rachel's. This one is Jamie's."

She turned and gestured to the door next to her son's on the other side. "And mine is there. The rest are for guests, and that one in the middle opens onto the staircase to the attic. I keep it locked so my son doesn't try to explore by himself. The steps are steep."

Chase decided to start with her room. He expected Kate to leave him to check on Jamie, but instead she followed him through the door.

When he entered her tastefully decorated bedroom, he immediately saw her touches throughout, from the family photos on the dresser and nightstands, to a gavel attached to a plaque on the wall.

"That's from my first case as a judge. My husband had it mounted and gave it to me as a surprise. He'd told me he was also going to do the gavel of my last trial, so I would have matching plaques. I intend to fulfill his wish."

"Does this incident make you think twice about being a judge?"

She cocked her head. "I don't think so. There are risks in a lot of people's jobs. You should know that more than anyone. Have you ever considered giving up being a police officer because of the risks?"

He hadn't thought about it, either, but now that he did, the answer that came to mind surprised him. "I've been the first person to go into a dangerous situation plenty of times—but better me than some of the other guys. I don't have a family, and a lot of my fellow officers do. If something happened to me, it wouldn't affect a wife or children."

"So you never want to get married and have a family?"

Want? Want had nothing to do with it. What right did he have to build a family when so many good men had been forced to leave their loved ones behind forever? He'd walked away from an ambush alive while all the men with families had been killed. His friend who had taught him about God had died in that firefight and fallen on top of him. In the end, that was what had saved him. Later, he'd known the pain and grief his buddy's wife had gone through, but he could do little to change that. He hated that feeling of impotency and had promised himself he would protect others at all costs.

"I'm sorry. You don't have to answer that. It isn't in your job description." She walked into her closet.

"I don't mind. Starting a family's just not in my plans right now." He headed for the first window, checked it, then moved to the other one. "Both are locked. I'll finish with the rest of the house."

She emerged from her closet. "I hope you'll have dinner with us. It's nothing fancy. It's a Mexican chicken dish. On Saturday and Sunday, I cook up a storm then we eat the meals throughout the week." She grinned. "I've been accused of being highly organized."

"Thanks. I skipped lunch today working a burglary case. I've been accused of being highly determined."

"To the point of going without food?"

He nodded then left before he became distracted from his task. Kate could easily do that with one look or smile.

After she took a quick shower and dressed, she stopped by Jamie's bedroom again. When she cracked the door open and looked inside, she found her son standing up in his crib and lifting his leg to try and climb out. He'd succeeded a couple of times. She crossed to him and swung him up into her arms.

"I should have known you wouldn't sleep through to

the morning." She hugged him against her, wishing she could stay like this the whole night.

"Mama, me eat."

"So you're hungry. No wonder you woke up." She headed for the hallway. "Let's go get you something for dinner."

"Down. Down." He wiggled in her arms.

"Not until we get to the kitchen." When Jamie was awake, they locked a gate across the bottom or top of the staircase. He was still a little shaky on the steps. She reached the first floor and put the barrier in place. She didn't need to worry anymore about him than she already had today.

The second she entered the kitchen she put Jamie on the floor, expecting him to make a beeline for his high chair and climb up into his seat. When he was hungry, that was what he usually did. But he stopped after two steps and stared at Chase across the room. Then he struck out for him and threw his arms around his leg.

Jamie loved meeting new people, but after today, she'd thought that might be different. She hadn't known he'd really been aware of the man who had saved them today, but he must have been because he raised his hands, opening and closing them.

"Up!"

Chase hoisted Jamie into his arms. "Sure, big guy. I'm Chase. I have a nephew not too much older than you."

"Case." Her son rubbed his hand across Chase's day-old beard. He giggled and did it again.

Seeing Jamie with Chase made her realize her son didn't have too many males in his life. She closed the space between the police detective and her. "C'mon, Jamie. Time to eat." As Rachel put the food on the table, Kate took him from Chase and set her son in his high chair.

After everyone was seated, Kate bowed her head and said, "Lord, thank You for sending us Chase when we needed him. Bless this food and our soldiers protecting us. Amen."

When she looked up, Chase was staring at her, and for a few seconds her son and Rachel faded into the background, the lure of his gaze making her forget who else was around. No wonder she'd remembered him from all the many people who frequented the county courthouse. It wasn't just that he was handsome—there was also an intensity to him that drew her attention. When he'd described himself as determined, she understood why. There was something about the man that intrigued her.

A purring Boss rubbing against her leg pulled her attention back to the moment.

While Rachel was eating, Kate assisted Jamie with his meal, a mixture of baby food and the Mexican chicken, trying to minimize Jamie's chances to play with it or fling it. Then her nanny would take over while Kate had her dinner. But her son kept getting distracted by Chase across the table from him—probably because he was the first man to sit at her table. She hadn't realized how small her world had become since Jamie's birth.

Her world centered around her child, the only one she would ever have. For ten years she and her husband had tried to have a baby. She had miscarried four times, and they'd given up the last year James was alive. Then her husband had died in a small plane crash. Not long after his death, she'd discovered she was pregnant. James would never know he had a son. A complication after Jamie's birth had led to a hysterectomy. Jamie would be her only child, but she cherished him and thanked the Lord for her one baby.

Jamie flipped his spoon, causing his food to fly in several directions.

"Okay. That's my sign you're finished." Kate took the utensil and bowl off the tray while Boss licked the food that landed on the tiled floor.

Then her son rubbed his eyes and tried to stand in his seat. Kate rose and picked him up. She noticed her nanny was finished with her meal and said, "After you wash him up, let's try and put him to bed again."

Rachel stood and took Jamie from Kate. "I'm surprised he even woke up after not sleeping much last night. I'll take care of him. You need to eat."

When the nanny left the kitchen with Jamie, Kate served several spoons of her Mexican chicken onto her plate. "Do you want anymore?"

"Yes. I don't get a lot of home-cooked food. This is delicious."

Kate passed the serving spoon to Chase. Their fingers briefly touched. For a few seconds she forgot to breathe. Sharing a meal with a man was something she hadn't done in so long she didn't know how to react anymore. She sternly reminded herself not to be silly. This wasn't a date—he was just trying to keep her and her son safe. If an assailant wanted to hurt her, the most effective way would be to do something to Jamie. Zed Hammer's anger the last day she saw him might have driven him to harm her son. The thought plunged fear deeper into her. She'd fought to have her son, and she would fight to keep him and protect him from any harm.

"Is the house secure?"

"All windows and doors are locked. You have a good security system, but vigilance is important, too."

"Now I wish I had a big dog. Would it be good to get

one tomorrow? I'll do whatever I need to make sure Jamie is all right."

"If you got a dog tomorrow, it would take some time to train him properly. Right now you need a guard dog. I could loan you Mac. He's a German shepherd. When I got him, he'd been a guard dog. He's well-trained, or I wouldn't offer."

A German shepherd she hadn't raised? She didn't know if that would be a good idea, and yet having him might be just what she needed at this time. "On one condition. Would you stay with us for the day after bringing him to make sure Mac is a fit for us? I know that's asking a lot, but I need to be assured Mac won't have any problems with Jamie, Rachel and me, not to mention my cat. Have you ever loaned him out before?"

"No, and that's a good suggestion. Tomorrow is Saturday. I can bring him by in the morning and introduce you to Mac."

"Good. I'd like that." But this incident made her realize she needed a dog as a permanent pet. Jamie would love it.

Chase's cell phone rang. "I need to answer this. It's my partner." He pushed to his feet and walked into the hallway.

Kate tried to eat a few bites of her dinner, but knots of tension riddled her stomach. She finally decided not to force it down. As she began taking the dishes to the sink, Chase reentered the kitchen.

"Was it about Zed Hammer?"

"Yes. We got a search warrant for his house. I'm meeting my partner over there. I'll have a patrol car drive by your place at least once an hour. With the police force looking for the car and Hammer, hopefully we'll find him soon. In the meantime, I hope we'll get some useful data from his home. If he's the attacker, then I want to have solid evidence against him."

For a second, she wanted to ask him to stay, but he was right that his duty lay elsewhere. Her house was secured, and she wanted the person responsible in jail tonight, if possible.

She went to her desk and jotted her cell phone number on a piece of paper. "Call me if you find anything."

He checked his watch. "It could be late."

"I don't care. I'd like to know."

He pocketed the scrap of paper she gave him and offered her his business card in return. "Okay, I will."

Kate walked with him to the foyer and turned off the alarm. "Thank you for all you've done today. I hate to think what could have happened if you hadn't shown up." A shudder rippled through her.

At the front door, Chase paused and turned. "You have my number. Call if you need me. Any time, day or night. I don't live far from here. I can be here in ten minutes."

"I appreciate it." She gave him a smile.

When he left, she locked up and turned on the alarm again. Then she glanced around, realizing how big the house was. But Chase had checked it. If someone came in through a door or window, the alarm would go off. After cleaning the dishes, she headed upstairs.

Rachel backed out of Jamie's room and quietly closed the door, then swung around. "I think he's officially asleep this time. I waited awhile to make sure."

"Thanks. I'm going to bed, too. Long day."

"Don't worry about Jamie. I have the monitor on, and if he wakes up, I'll hear and check on him. Get some rest."

That was easier said than done, Kate noted later as she stared up at her dark ceiling. She was exhausted but not sleepy. She was glad tomorrow was a day off. Maybe before the weekend was over, her attacker would be found, and she could make up for the sleep she'd lost. Her docket was full next week.

Finally her eyelids grew heavy. She hugged her pillow and began to drift off.

Until the sound of a siren penetrated her mind.

She sat up and listened, her heartbeat pounding. The noise faded into the distance, and she sighed. She was overreacting. This was ridiculous.

With a glance at the clock, she settled again under the covers. It was after midnight. Like her son, she'd gotten little rest last night. Centering her thoughts on the Lord watching over her, she finally fell asleep...

The high-pitched sound of her alarm jerked her awake.

# THREE

Chase stood next to his partner, Todd Grayson, in Hammer's living room and frowned. Nothing.

"We still have the garage, and the tech guys will go through his computer," Todd said.

"Where is this guy if he isn't guilty?"

"We'll find him and ask him that question. He has a motive. His car, which wasn't reported stolen, was the getaway vehicle. He has a lot of explaining."

Chase started for the kitchen. "Let's check the garage then go home. Tomorrow I'll interview the couple of neighbors who weren't home earlier. Maybe someone will know where he is."

"I'll interview Hammer's ex-wife and boss. Something will turn up."

In the meantime, Kate was scared for her child. He'd investigated a couple of kidnappings since he'd returned to the police force two years ago. He'd seen the terror and heartache the parents went through, especially with the one that ended tragically. He wished at times he could turn off his emotions totally. Usually he managed to push them down enough so he could work effectively on the case. He wasn't so sure he could manage that this time.

There was something about Kate that pulled at him.

When fighting the attacker, she'd been ferocious. But the second Jamie was safe, her tenderness had surged to the foreground as she comforted her son.

"I'll take the left side," Chase said and moved to a group of stacked boxes.

Kate had Rachel, but she didn't have any family here. She was essentially alone. That thought knocked holes in the barrier he'd erected around his heart. His only mission, especially since he'd survived the ambush, had been to protect and serve others.

The blare of his cell phone cut through the silence in the garage. He saw it was Kate's number, and his pulse picked up speed. Was Hammer there?

He punched the accept button. "Detective Walker here," he said in his professional voice, trying to keep that wall between them.

"My alarm is going off. Someone must be in the house."

"Did you call 9-1-1?" Chase headed for the garage door button to raise it.

"You *are* 9-1-1."

"I'll be right there. Get Jamie and Rachel and lock yourselves in the bathroom. I'll be there as soon as I can." He hit the opener.

"Hurry."

"I will. Stay on the phone with me." Then to his partner who held some photos he'd found, he said, "Judge Forster's alarm went off."

As Chase jogged to his car, Todd shouted, "I'm coming, right behind you. I'll let the station know."

"Do you have Jamie yet?" Chase asked Kate as he slipped behind his steering wheel.

"Yes," she said in a breathless voice. "Rachel's here, too. We'll be in the main upstairs bathroom." Fear dripped off each word.

The sound ripped through his heart. He dug deep to remain calm and remember what he'd learned in his hostage negotiation class. He started his car and floored it. "I'm coming. Get away from the door in the bathroom, if possible."

Kate spoke to Rachel about what to do. "We're in the tub." He barely heard what she said over Jamie's crying. A pause then she said, "Jamie, Chase is coming. We're going to be all right, honey."

Jamie's crying quieted. Chase imagined Kate gently rocking her son as she'd done at the reserve.

"See Case?"

"Yes. You remember him from earlier tonight."

A smile tugged at Chase's mouth as he stopped at the gate and put in the number she'd given him earlier. He drummed his fingers against the steering wheel as the wrought-iron barricade slowly moved out of the way.

When he was inside, he texted the code to Todd then said to Kate, "I'm here. Still all right?"

"Yes. The alarm is still blaring, but that's all I can hear."

"Let's hope it only malfunctioned."

She chuckled, a bit shaky. "Better than someone here."

As he hurried toward the large house, he said, "I need to pocket my phone to free up my hands, but I won't disconnect." He hated not to have that connection with her, but his focus had to be totally on what was going on.

As he approached the porch, he continually scanned the area around him. The noise from the alarm constantly reminded him that Kate, Jamie and Rachel were in danger. His gaze latched onto a broken windowpane at the far end of the long porch. Was that the only reason the alarm had gone off? As Todd and another patrol car pulled up to her house, he withdrew his phone.

"Someone broke a lower windowpane in the living room."

After she told Rachel, she asked, "Do you want me to come downstairs and turn the alarm off then open the door?"

"Not until I have gone around the house and checked for any other attempts to get inside."

"The alarm must have scared the person off."

He hoped that was the case. "I don't want to bust your door down unless necessary. Hang on. I'll let you know what to do."

"Actually I have a key hidden outside in the rock garden." She described the exact location. "My security code is 6735."

"I don't think it's a good idea to keep a key outside."

"I know. Honestly, I forgot about it. After James died, I was forgetful and locked myself out of the house twice. I put a key in the garden so I didn't need a locksmith to come to my house anymore. Strangely once I did, I never had to use it."

"Good." He walked to the spot and bent down to retrieve the key. "I've got it. I'm pocketing my cell phone. Don't open the bathroom door unless it's me."

Todd joined him. "You think that's it?"

"I hope so. But if someone wanted to break a window to get into the house, why the front porch with the security lights on in front?"

While Todd went to the left, Chase moved right, that question plaguing him.

Sitting in the dry bathtub facing Rachel, Kate gently rocked Jamie back and forth. He was fighting going to sleep. She began singing a soft lullaby. Jamie's eyes finally slid all the way closed.

"I think he's going back to sleep," Kate whispered to Rachel while glancing at her watch. It had been ten minutes since Chase began checking out the rest of the house. Ten *long* minutes.

"Good." Rachel looked at Jamie. "He has to be exhausted."

"So am I, but I've got a feeling tonight won't be a restful one."

Rachel smiled. "I know what you mean."

"I'm so glad I have you to help." Without her husband, she'd felt so lost and grief-stricken until her nanny was hired. Kate hoped this problem didn't drive Rachel away. "When this is over with, I'm going to rearrange my schedule so you can have a vacation, my treat."

"Really? Thanks! My brother moved to Seattle a few months back, and I've wanted to see that area of the country."

"Are you close to your brother?"

"We were growing up but not now. Too many miles between us. We chat on the computer, but it isn't the same."

"I know what you mean." She again glanced at her watch. "Maybe I'll take Jamie to Florida to my mom's and grandmother's." Hiding from a possible intruder caused her to reevaluate her priorities. She loved her job, but it wasn't the most important thing in her life. God and her family were. She was all Jamie had and vice versa.

When her phone rang, the sound startled her and Kate jumped. Jamie opened his eyes for a few seconds then went back to sleep while she answered the call.

"Is everything clear?" she asked Chase.

"Except for a rock in the living room, yes. Todd and I have gone through the rooms downstairs. I'll be there shortly. You still okay?"

"Yes, especially now."

When she ended the call, she peered at Rachel, tense and intent. "It doesn't look like anyone got inside. All they've found is a rock thrown through the window."

Putting her hand over her heart, her nanny wilted, finally relaxing against the side of the tub.

"Remind me to call the alarm company tomorrow," Kate said.

"Believe me, I will. You don't think the rock was a prank, do you? There are a couple of teenage boys who get a little rowdy in the neighborhood."

Rachel often took Jamie to a small park nearby and would end up talking with other nannies. "Have you heard of any others having a rock thrown at their house?"

Rachel scrunched her forehead. "Well, no, not exactly. More like tossing water balloons then running away."

A moment later, there was a knock on the door. "Kate, it's Chase. It's all clear."

"Now that's music to my ears," she said loud enough for him to hear.

Rachel climbed out of the tub then lifted Jamie into her arms while Kate rose.

"Please make sure Jamie goes down, then get some sleep yourself." Kate went first, unlocked the door and opened it.

The first thing she saw was Chase's smile. She had to fight the urge to hug the police detective. "Thank you for coming so fast."

"What else could I do? I've never been someone's 9-1-1 call." His grin widened.

"I'm hoping that's my last one." But she didn't want it to be the last time she saw him. The thought surprised her. Since James's death, all she'd done was work and be the best mom she could. She neither needed nor wanted another relationship in her life…right?

Rachel nodded at Chase while she scurried toward Jamie's bedroom.

When her nanny and son were gone, she started for the stairs. "Show me where the rock came in."

"It's in the living room." He gave her the key he'd used. "My partner has some wood we can put over the window for a temporary fix."

"Who's your partner?" she asked at the bottom of the steps.

"Todd Grayson. He helped me clear the house. Two patrol officers are outside—one in the back and the other in the front." As Kate entered the living room, Chase quickly added, "Watch your step—I haven't processed the scene yet."

She assessed the damaged window, the glass littering the floor and the good-size rock. "What are you hoping to find?"

"Maybe fingerprints from the rock. I know you don't have any video surveillance, but do any of your neighbors have cameras?"

"I don't know. Tomorrow I'll be getting cameras added for security, but I'm not sure what to do until then."

"If you want, when my partner comes back, I'll go home and bring Mac over now then stay the rest of the night."

"But what about your sleep?"

"I can stretch out on the couch. It'll give me a chance to talk to your neighbors first thing in the morning. Is Jamie all right? Did he sleep through it?"

"He woke up, but I was able to get him to go back to sleep." His presence calmed her nerves. "Did you find anything at Zed Hammer's house?"

"No, but we still have the garage to finish. We were partway through the search when you called. Todd told me he would go back and finish after we take care of your window."

"I'm going to make a pot of coffee. Do you want any?"

"Sounds good. I see my partner returning. We'll be on the porch nailing up the board then I'll go get Mac."

"Does your partner drink coffee?"

"Yes, black, no sugar, just like me."

Kate paused in the hallway and looked back at Chase leaving out the front door. *Lord, thank You for sending Chase. Please watch over Jamie. He's all I have.*

Chase drove into his garage, downed the last of his luke-warm coffee from Kate and climbed from his SUV. When he entered his kitchen, Mac greeted him, his tail wagging. He quickly fed him and gathered up his dog's supplies to take to Kate's place. Then, while Mac ate his late dinner, Chase hurried and took a shower then changed into jeans and a long-sleeve T-shirt.

As he walked back to the kitchen, he passed through the living room and realized there were only a few personal touches in his house. Nothing like Kate's, which was full of pictures of Jamie from a small baby to the present. The majority of her rooms had some kind of evidence a tod-dler lived in the home, from toys to a horse on wheels to the plug covers and padding on sharp furniture corners that she must have added to baby proof the house. Defi-nitely her home had the lived-in feel while his was a notch above a hotel suite.

After gathering what he needed to take to Kate's, he headed for his SUV and opened the back door for Mac. His dog barked once, excited about being in the car. Adopting Mac had been the only thing he'd done for himself since he returned to Cimarron City, and he wouldn't have even done that if a friend hadn't needed him to take the guard dog because he was moving overseas. His sterile lifestyle had kept him focused on his job and helping others. He wanted his survival to count for something.

When he arrived at Kate's and parked in her driveway, he scanned the house and street as he and his German shepherd made their way to the porch. He used her spare key she'd given back to him to let himself in, making his way toward the kitchen where he'd left Todd and Kate.

Soft, feminine laughter along with his partner's robust laugh drifted to Chase as he neared the room. Mac's ears perked at the sounds.

When Chase entered, Kate passed her cell phone to Todd. "This was Jamie's attempt at climbing the bookcase. Thankfully he only got to the second shelf before I discovered him. I left for a minute to get a book."

"He moves fast. That's what Sammy does. The second my wife and I take our eyes off him, he's into something he shouldn't be. I can't wait until he grows out of this inquisitive stage."

"I've read that might be years away." Kate's gaze lit upon Chase.

Todd groaned. "Don't tell me that. I just found out Peggy is pregnant with our second child." He twisted around and peered at Chase.

"I sent a patrol officer to keep an eye on Hammer's place until I could finish the search, so as much as I've enjoyed our little conversation, I need to get over there. I'll let you know if I find anything, Chase."

"Thanks for helping." Kate rose. "Do you want any more coffee to take with you?"

"Yes, I'd like that."

"Chase, how about you?"

"Sounds great. Can you come down to the police station and fix that every day for us? Yours is actually drinkable."

Kate refilled a paper coffee cup for Todd and handed it to him.

His partner grinned. "I'll lock the door as I leave."

Kate gave Chase his drink, then turned her attention to Mac. Holding her hand for the dog to smell, she said, "You're beauti—I mean, handsome, Mac."

Chase introduced Kate to his pet, then unhooked his leash and told him to sit and stay. "I'll be right back. I'm going to do a quick walk through downstairs to make sure everything is still locked up."

"I'll check the kitchen. Can I pet Mac?"

"Yes. I've let him know that you're a friend."

When he returned to the kitchen, Kate had seated herself in a chair near Mac and was petting him. Boss was on a chair asleep as if a strange dog in his house didn't mean anything.

She glanced up. "After making sure the kitchen was secured, I sat and tried to entice him to come to me. He didn't move so I did."

"He's well-trained. He doesn't respond to others giving him commands unless I work with you to do that."

"So if a burglar came in, he wouldn't stay put just because the intruder said to?"

"Right." He took a seat at the table. "You can go to bed if you want. You'll be safe tonight. The alarm is back on, everything is locked and Mac and I are here."

"I'm going to when I finish this coffee."

"It doesn't keep you up?"

She shifted around to face him. "No. Caffeine doesn't affect me like other people. I drink way too much, but I love the taste. One of my bad habits I need to do something about."

Chase chuckled. "If that's considered a bad habit, then I have more than I thought." He gave Mac the hand signal to rest by his chair. "But in my case, caffeine does keep me up. I figure I can sleep tomorrow after you're taken care of."

"So you don't want a blanket and pillow?"

"No. I might close my eyes, but I won't fall asleep. You should go ahead and rest. I'll be fine."

"Are you sure? You've gone above and beyond the call of duty."

"I'll do anything for a home-cooked meal. Your Mexican chicken was delicious."

Kate tried to suppress a yawn but couldn't. "Then tomorrow you can't leave until I've fixed you a full breakfast. I love to cook."

"You're not getting an argument from me. I usually eat out so that'll be a treat."

Kate's eyelids slid halfway down.

"Go to bed before you fall asleep talking to me. I have a bum leg. I might not be able to carry you upstairs."

Her eyes popped open wide. "I'm okay." She covered her mouth and yawned again. "I'm going to bed."

He walked with her to the staircase.

On the first step, she turned. "I noticed when you ran after my attacker today that you were limping when you came back. What happened to your leg?"

For a few seconds he scrambled for what to say. He didn't talk about that last ambush with anyone. Then he stared into her beautiful eyes, and the words just came out. "I was shot while serving in the Marines." Then to play it down, he shrugged and added. "It happens in a war zone, but I'm fine now. It only acts up when I push myself too much."

"I'm sorry that happened today."

He needed to shut down this conversation now. "I'm sorry that you were attacked today." He grasped her hand.

"Go to sleep. See you in a few hours." When he released her hand, he missed touching her.

He distanced himself from her and watched her ascend the staircase. At the top, she glanced over her shoulder at him and smiled. When she disappeared from the landing, he stared at the place where she'd been seconds ago.

*What is it about Kate that intrigues me?*

He patted the side of his leg. "C'mon, Mac. We should try to relax at least."

As he entered the living room, his cell phone rang, and he quickly answered the call from his partner. "Did you find anything in the garage?"

"More than enough to arrest Hammer when we find him."

# FOUR

Having overslept, Kate hurried down the stairs to start breakfast before Rachel and Jamie awakened. She was glad they both had gotten needed rest. It had taken her over an hour to fall asleep, which would account for sleeping through the alarm.

When she peeked into the living room, expecting to see Chase and Mac, it was empty. The only thing that had finally allowed her to doze off was the thought they were downstairs protecting Jamie, Rachel and her. Did something happen?

For a moment, panic seized her as though she were in a tug-of-war again with her attacker. But she quickly squashed the fear. Chase was probably patrolling through the house. She hastened through the vacant rooms, then returned to the foyer to see if the alarm was still on. It wasn't.

Her heartbeat picked up with each second that passed. She crossed to the dining room window and peered between the slats in the blinds. Chase had Mac on a leash and was talking with Todd in the front yard. His partner handed Chase what looked like photos. Of Hammer's house? The getaway car? Another crime scene?

She started to go outside to see, but halfway to the door she decided not to. She needed to get breakfast ready. She'd promised Chase a special one, and she intended to deliver. It might be about another case. If it was concerning Jamie's attempted kidnapping yesterday, Chase would tell her when he came inside.

She walked to the kitchen and began preparing a quiche lorraine. After it was in the oven, she made coffee then sliced up strawberries, a cantaloupe and a pineapple then put them in the refrigerator. When she glanced at the clock over the stove, she realized it was well after eight o'clock. The alarm company had promised to be here by nine-thirty. Only an hour away. After what happened yesterday, she'd prefer not having anyone here, but the window and the alarm hooked to it had to be fixed.

"Why the frown?"

Chase's voice coming from the kitchen entrance startled her. She whirled around, laying her splayed hand over her chest. She hadn't heard him come into the house. How was she going to protect her son when she couldn't even notice intruders?

"Sorry. I didn't mean to scare you."

With her heartbeat thumping against her rib cage, she waved her hand in the air. "It was no big deal. I should have been listening more carefully. You might be used to being super vigilant. I'm not."

"You should be. You're a judge involved in the criminal system."

"I don't think of family court in the same way as criminal court."

"You should. When it comes to the family, emotions can be very heated and long-lasting. It becomes personal."

"You're right. My goal is always to protect the children and do what I can to keep the family together. When those are conflicting goals, the child's welfare comes first." She took plates down from the cabinet and crossed to the table.

"Can I help? I may not cook, but I know how to set the table."

"Sure. We're having quiche, fruit and cinnamon toast. Jamie loves it. I'm going to check on Jamie and Rachel. She should be up by now. Jamie probably is, too."

"Before you go, I want to show you copies of some pictures that were found at Hammer's house in the garage. We're hoping you can tell us when and where all of them were taken."

"Any news concerning Hammer?"

"No. Todd is checking with the neighbors about security cameras then he'll join us."

"Great. I have enough breakfast for him, too, if he wants any."

"Knowing my partner, he won't turn down a meal."

"Where's Mac? I saw you had him on a leash."

"I walked around the house to make sure I didn't miss anything last night in the dark then I put him in the backyard to exercise." He headed for the counter by the kitchen entrance and picked up a stack of photos. "You might want to sit. The idea of someone stalking you and taking the pictures can really hit home when you see them."

When she took a seat at the table, Chase passed them to her. A trembling in her hands quickly spread throughout her body as she shuffled through the ten pictures, highlighting different aspects of her day from running with Jamie to grocery shopping to being at the courthouse.

The last one was taken at the Remington Nature Reserve as she was getting out of the car. The jogging clothes she had on were what she'd worn the day before the attempted kidnapping. Chills flashed up her spine while sweat beaded on her forehead and upper lip.

She pointed to that photo. "He must have been at the reserve on Thursday. That's what I wore, and it was cloudy like that at the time we went."

"The others? When do you think they were taken?"

"This week." She sorted them by what she had on. "Those two Monday morning. These Tuesday afternoon and the rest Thursday throughout the day. And I didn't notice anything unusual." Sweat rolled into her eye, and she swiped it away.

Chase gathered the pictures. "Thanks. When we find Hammer, this will help us with what questions to ask him. We'll also try to figure out where Hammer was those days and if he has an alibi. Of course, we could catch a break, and he'll confess."

She rose. "I'd better go upstairs and get Rachel. The quiche will be ready in a few minutes. If the timer goes off while I'm gone, please turn off the heat and take it out of the oven."

"I will and I'll finish setting the table. Do you want me to do anything for the cinnamon toast?"

"It's set up to go. I'll do that at the last minute." Kate hurried from the kitchen, needing to get away from those photos. The knowledge the kidnapping had been planned for days, if not longer, made the situation even more serious to her.

Later, after the man who replaced the window glass and the technician from the alarm company had left Kate's house, Chase walked with his partner toward his car. "I wonder if Hammer has fled Cimarron City since his attempt failed."

"Even if he left, his photo and license plate numbers have been sent to every county in Oklahoma. Hopefully something will come from widening the search." Todd stopped at his sedan and twisted toward Chase. "How did she take the photos?"

"About as well as you would think." Chase could still remember her hands shaking and the color leaching from her face. Chase had wanted to promise he wouldn't let anything happen to her or Jamie, but he could never guarantee that. He didn't want to give her false hope. She needed to be as vigilant as possible.

"I wondered, because she didn't say too much through breakfast."

"And she held Jamie rather than put him in his highchair. She kept looking at one of the pictures."

"The photo of her standing at the window holding Jamie?" Todd leaned against his car, crossing his arms and ankles.

"Yup."

"What are you going to do? Leave Mac here?"

"After the rock incident, I'm staying even if I have to sit out in front of her house. I wonder if the rock was thrown to test her security system." Chase lounged against Todd's car and stared at Kate's house.

"That's possible. I wish the two neighbors' cameras hadn't been covered."

"The fact that he knew who had cameras is just another thing to indicate he's been casing her for a while." Every time he thought of the extent of planning the attacker had gone to, Chase's gut knotted like a hard fist.

"I hope you don't have to resort to sleeping in your SUV. A couch is a lot more comfortable. If anything comes up, I'll let you know. Maybe Hammer's car will be found, and he'll be inside."

"We can always hope. Talk to you later." Chase shoved away from Todd's sedan and started for Kate's house.

When he entered, he retrieved Mac from the backyard

then put the alarm in stay mode. He'd already told Kate and Rachel he would. Everyone was in the den, trying to act as if there was nothing wrong. Jamie sat on the floor, playing with his big blocks. Boss was sunning himself on a table near the window.

The second he spied Mac coming into the room, Jamie pushed himself to his feet. "Doggie." A huge grin spread across his chubby cheeks, and he half walked, half ran toward the German shepherd.

"Mac, sit." Chase knelt next to his pet.

Kate made her way to her son and slowed his steps by taking his arm. "Jamie, you need to be gentle with the doggie. Running at him could scare him." Crouching on the other side of Mac, she raised his hand and ran it along the back of the dog. "Nice and easy. Mac loves to be rubbed here." Kate showed Jamie the sweet spot on the dog's neck.

"Mac likes that. See his tail wagging?" Chase pointed to it swishing back and forth in the doorway.

"Like doggie."

Before anyone could stop Kate's son, he laid his head against Mac, caressing his cheek. Chase could remember how much he'd loved his dog when he was growing up. They went everywhere together.

Jamie put his arms around Mac. "My doggie."

Kate looked at Chase. He gave her a slight nod to show that she should handle this. She said to Jamie, "Hon, Mac is Chase's dog. He's loaning us the dog for a few days. He heard how much you love animals and thought you would enjoy having Mac here."

Jamie lifted his head and switched his attention between her and Chase. "Me love Mac." He ran his hand along the dog's back. "See?"

"I do. Would you like to throw a ball for Mac to fetch?

He loves to play that game." Chase rose. "If your mom says it's okay, we can go out back."

His eyes as round as saucers, Jamie twisted toward Kate. "Go now."

"It sounds like a great idea. Rachel, would you please fix lunch?" Kate pushed to her feet.

"Yes, we still have chicken salad. I'll make some sandwiches."

"Let us know when it's time to eat." Kate started to take Jamie's hand.

Instead, her son moved to Mac's side and settled his touch on the dog's back. He talked to Mac, most of what he said being unintelligible. But there were a few words Chase understood sprinkled throughout the conversation.

In the middle of the fenced-in backyard, Jamie remained at the dog's side and held out his arm. "Ball."

Chase had snatched it from Mac's things in the kitchen as they passed through a minute ago. "Do you know how to throw a ball?"

Kate laughed. "He loves to throw one, not necessarily accurately."

Chase closed the space between him and the boy and knelt next to him. When he gave Jamie the tennis ball, it left the child's hand before Chase could give him pointers. The ball bounced five feet to the side. Mac looked at Chase then moseyed over to it and picked it up then came back and dropped it at Jamie's feet. The boy giggled and tried again.

Chase moved back to Kate. "Jamie has his own method."

"Haphazard, yes."

After a few pitches, Jamie decided to change things up. He would send the ball sailing, then ran after it with Mac. At first, Chase stepped nearer, not sure how his dog would deal with competition, but soon Mac turned it into a game. Sometimes he would get the prize while other times he'd let Jamie get it.

"Mac is great with little children." Kate closed the space between them.

"My friend who gave me Mac had children. I never thought to ask him about how Mac would be with kids."

"A natural. It's like he knows Jamie is young and needs gentleness and patience."

"Animals sense a lot of things." When Chase had had one of his nightmares about that last skirmish and had woken up shaking and sweating, Mac had been right there to comfort him. In the past months, he'd had fewer of those dark dreams and part of the reason was Mac.

"I feel comfortable with Mac here. When the workers were fixing the alarm and window, he sat nearby and watched their every move. I'm glad we didn't have to find out what he'd do if one of them stepped out of line."

"He'd corner the person. Unless physically threatened, he'd just remind them he was there and prepared to protect."

Kate pointed at his dog sitting on the ground letting Jamie rub him. "As fierce as he can seem, you wouldn't expect that kind of gentleness from him."

"He's been trained and treated well. Speaking of Mac, I wanted to talk to you about me staying here until Hammer is caught, too. My dog is good, but I'd feel better if I was here. The couch was quite comfortable, and I even dozed some last night."

She released a slow breath. "I wasn't going to ask you, but with both of you here, I'd feel even better and safer. I'm so glad you want to. But what about your work and Monday when I go back to court? I'm concerned about Jamie's safety here in the house with just Rachel."

"I'm hoping we'll find Hammer by then, but if we don't,

we'll discuss it then. I'm thinking my younger brother, who is a police officer, could help with Jamie or I'll check with my chief about assigning a uniform to be here with Rachel and your son. I could drive you to and from the courthouse to make sure you're safe and to check in with the security guards there. That way I can work on the case. Todd is doing the legwork right now. We want to have enough evidence to charge Hammer and keep him in jail without bail. The photos at his house will help us a lot. And when we find his car, there might be more evidence to tie him to the attack." He took her hand. "Don't worry. We'll get him. His photo has been circulated everywhere. The news network has picked it up and has shown it several times in the last twenty-four hours."

Kate faced him, only a foot between them. Her brown eyes fastened onto him, and he felt a new and somewhat unsettling sense of connection toward her.

He dropped her hand and stepped back. He needed to remain detached and on guard. "I'll stay until Hammer is caught," he said to remind himself he was unofficially on duty.

"Jamie finally went down for a nap," Kate said on Sunday as she came into the den where Chase was going through her list of cases from the last few years.

"I need your input. Did any of these people make threats against you or make you uncomfortable?"

Kate sat next to Chase to go through the files he had already perused. "Find anyone promising besides Hammer?"

"A couple we'll look into, but most would do something not long after the event that angered them. That doesn't mean a person can't hold a grudge and wait, but it's not as likely. Hammer still is our best option. Men with a known pattern of domestic violence, which is the reason you limited his visitation with his children, are volatile. Tempers flare easily, especially if he thinks he's wronged."

"The abuse was directed only at his wife. His children wanted to see their father so I came up with a supervised visitation plan with a case worker so the mother wouldn't be involved. I feel both parents are important to a child's emotional growth, but sometimes I've had to completely deny a parent visitation rights."

"Any in the last year?"

"There was one last fall. Let me see if I can find his folder." Kate dug through the stack until she found Dale Winn. "Here it is. Not a nice man."

"I'll have Todd check him out. I'll put him at the top of my list of people requiring further investigation."

"Where's your list?"

Chase passed the pad he'd been using to Kate. She let out a sound of surprise. "It's a long list."

"You're one busy judge."

She nodded her agreement. "Sadly, my docket is full. I wish it wasn't. James and I had a great relationship and wanted to have several children. We tried. I miscarried four times. We'd come to the realization that adoption might be the best option for us. Not long after James died, I discovered I was pregnant. I honestly didn't know if I would make it past three months. But I did." When she thought back to that long month wondering if she would miscarry again, her emotions were all over the place. "When I was six-months pregnant, I realized my dream of having my husband's child might come true." Her throat closed around that last word, and she looked away from the sympathy in Chase's expression.

He laid a hand on her shoulder. "I've had days when I didn't want to wake up and face the day. After the second surgery on my leg…"

His voice trailed off, and she blinked her tears away and twisted toward him. "What happened?"

He pulled his hand away. "I don't like to talk about it."

"I understand. I don't like to relive the months I knew I was going to have a baby and James wasn't there to celebrate with me. It was bittersweet. I was given the most precious baby, but I'd lost my husband. Finally, I realized by sharing with others I healed faster. We aren't meant to go through ordeals alone. We were made to help and support each other." She wouldn't force him, but she hoped he would tell her. She might be able to help him. "I'm here to listen if you ever want to."

"I appreciate the offer. What I went through was different."

"How was it?"

"I lost my best friend. We'd served together for several years and had gone through a lot."

"I lost my best friend, too. James and I went through so much together although not in a war zone. He was there for me when my father passed away, when I miscarried each time. I understand loss. The emptiness. The hole in your life that you don't know if you can ever fill. How did it happen?"

"We were ambushed by the enemy. He was right beside me one second, helping me because I was shot—" he snapped his fingers "—then the next second, he fell against me."

"That's how you hurt your leg?"

He nodded, swallowing hard several times.

"What was his name?"

For a long moment he didn't say anything, then whispered in a raspy voice, "T. J. Boone. He left a wife and two kids."

"I'm so sorry. Did he live here?"

"No, Dallas. Afterward, his wife moved back to her hometown in Oregon. I talk with her on the phone every now and then to make sure she's all right. Her family is very supportive and have helped her through her husband's death."

"But no one was there for you."

"It's not the same thing."

"Yes, it is. Whether you lose a close friend or a family member, you still go through the stages of grief. You still have to deal with the fact you'll never see him again."

As she waited, hoping he would share more, the doorbell chimed. The sound surprised her, and she gasped. "I'm not expecting anyone." She started to rise.

"I'll answer it."

She walked with him to the foyer, but she hung back while he checked the peephole.

The tense set to his shoulders eased. "It's Todd and my brother, Chad." He swung the door open. "What brings you all by? Have you found Hammer?"

"No, but his car was discovered in the woods outside town. Chad is gonna stay with Kate while you come with me. The patrol officer called to the scene said there is evidence in the vehicle. Clothes. A ski mask."

"Go. You might find something that tells you where Hammer is." Kate grinned at his younger brother. "Besides, it gives me time to pump—or rather, to get to know Chad."

"Okay." Then to his brother, Chase, said, "I'm counting on you. If Hammer dumped his car, he must know that we're on to him. Desperation might make him attack." He frowned. "On second thought, maybe you should go alone, Todd."

"Chase, I'm not gonna let you down." Chad stepped into the entry hall, his hand on the butt of his gun in its holster.

"You know what the attacker was wearing. You need to go. I'll be okay with Chad." Then Kate leaned closer and whispered, "I'd feel better if you were there while the car was processed. Please."

"You're right. Let's go, Todd." Chase paused by his brother. "I know you're capable."

The second Chase closed the door behind him mixed feelings surged through Kate. In a short time, she'd come to depend on him. What if something happened to him? Dumping the car where Hammer had to know it would be found very quickly seemed suspicious to her. Was it a trap? An ambush like three years ago?

# FIVE

The same white sedan Chase had seen leaving the parking lot at the Remington Nature Reserve sat nestled in brush in the woods outside of town. Was the greenery around the vehicle an attempt to disguise its location? A stiff wind had exposed the car or they might not have discovered it.

The officer guarding the scene disconnected his cell phone and met Chase and Todd partway on one of the paths not heavily used. "Two kids found it about an hour ago."

"Did they disturb it in any way, Officer Brown?" Chase asked, continuing toward the sedan.

"Yes, they moved some of the branches." The young man pointed to limbs tossed to the left.

Todd circled the area. "Did you call for a tow truck?"

"Yes," Officer Brown said. "Now that you're here, I'll go to the highway and make sure the guy knows where to turn."

After donning gloves, Chase pulled the greenery off the car until he could open the driver's door and lean in to examine the front. On the passenger side floor lay a black ski mask. Before he went around to take a closer look, he squatted to check around the driver's side more thoroughly. He spied a white slip of paper and carefully withdrew it from between the console and the cushion.

He read the words scribbled down on the note then he'd put it in a plastic bag, "Turn left at the big B, go three miles, make a right then almost immediately another one."

Todd lifted the trunk while Chase skirted the vehicle. "Must be directions somewhere."

"Yeah, but where? A big *B*? What in the world does that mean?" Chase continued to the passenger's front door.

"When we leave, we may have to look in the area for a big B. Maybe it's the name of a business."

Chase bagged the ski mask. "Or a wild goose chase."

Todd held up a length of rope. "You think his plan was to use this to tie someone up with?"

The twine dangling from his partner's hand stirred the anger he was trying to keep suppressed. Rope for Jamie or Kate or both? He shuddered at the thought of either one tied up. Good thing Hammer wasn't there right now.

By the time they finished investigating, taking fingerprints off various surfaces and bagging evidence, the tow truck appeared and began hooking the car up to haul to the police compound.

Chase stood back while the tow truck left the scene. "From what I've seen, it only looks like one set of prints inside the car. They have to be Hammer's. We can verify them with the ones found in his house." Some of the fingerprints were smudged but that was to be expected.

"Another piece of the evidence to nail the guy." His partner slid a look at him. "I can see why you've taken a personal interest in making sure Kate and her son are safe."

"And why's that?"

"Well, I could say she's an attractive, single lady in trouble, which is true, but I've seen how you are with my kid. You're a natural to be a dad. Not to mention, you could use a good woman in your life."

Chase pivoted toward Todd. "What's that supposed to mean?"

"It's not good being a loner, especially being a cop. We need that connection to family and someone we love. It keeps us grounded in what's worth fighting for. I know between your brother's and my families you get a taste of it, but believe me, it's not the same thing as the real deal."

Chase wanted to put an end to this conversation, but what Todd had said was partially true. He did yearn for a family and a wife at times, but he never wanted to cause grief like T.J. had when he'd left his wife behind. His death had crippled her. She'd tried to commit suicide. If Chase hadn't found her, she would have left her kids without a mother or father. And although he wasn't in a war zone like before, his job was dangerous. No, it was better if he yearned from afar.

"Let's go find what the big *B* means." Chase took out his cell phone to let Chad know what he was doing.

After putting Jamie down for a nap, Kate locked the gate on the second floor, then started down the stairs. Chase's brother's voice caught her attention.

"Nothing has happened here. You can stop worrying." Chad walked from the back of house into the foyer. He glanced up at her as he ended the call.

"Was that Chase? Did they find Hammer's car?"

"Yeah. He's following a clue he found at the scene."

Chase must be all right then—at least so far. She wanted him to find her attacker, and yet she didn't want anything to happen to him. "What clue?"

"Something about a sign with a big letter *B* on it. It might lead to the suspect."

A big *B*? By the woods and lake? She should know it. She grew up in Cimarron City and often stayed at the lake in the summer, especially as a child. But the mention of a big *B* didn't ring any bells. "I hope it does. I want him caught and my life back." She continued toward the kitchen, trying to remember what she knew about a big *B*.

As she chopped up the potatoes then carrots for the beef stew she was making, she decided to bake some honey-glazed biscuits to go on the side. Jamie loved the biscuits just like his dad had. It was the closest thing she came to preparing a dessert.

When it was time for her to get the ingredients for her biscuits out, she grabbed the honey from her pantry and suddenly remembered what the big *B* sign meant. Not the singular letter but a picture of a large bee smiling on a sign. When she was a child, her mother had bought her honey from the couple who had bees near the lake on the other side from where Chase had found the car.

Grabbing her phone, she called Chase.

When he answered the first thing he said was, "Is everything all right?"

"Yes. We're fine. Have you found the sign?"

"Not yet. When we left the scene, Todd went one way on the road and I went the opposite. So far nothing with a big *B*."

"That's because you're looking on the wrong part of the lake. Go to the west side. There is a couple who has bees and sells their honey. I haven't been out there in a few years, but there was a big sign with a bee on it. Actually, it used to scare me as a little girl. It's about in the middle of Lake Road."

"I'll let Todd know, and we'll go over there."

"Be safe," she said before she could censor herself. She cared about Chase, more than she should. He was only helping her because she was a judge.

"I'll be fine. Don't worry."

She didn't say anything for a few seconds.

"Okay, Kate?"

"Yes." *If I can just stop worrying.* "See you later."

When she hung up, she stared down at her phone, tempted to call him back just to hear his voice.

Suddenly the memory of the time her doorbell rang that changed her life flooded her mind. The highway patrol officer who had been on her porch hated to inform her that James had been in a small plane crash and the ambulance was taking him to the hospital. Before she had had a chance to go to James, the patrol officer called her to say he died en route to the emergency room. His voice had held sympathy and concern, but she hadn't remembered anything after she heard the word *died*.

When she answered the phone, she'd never thought she would hear those words. James and she had had such plans—all of them falling apart with that call. Could she ever put herself in a position to be hurt like that again?

As Chase approached the cabin, he observed a motorcycle parked out front. He hid behind some brush to case the area with his binoculars. The blinds were all pulled closed. Except for the bike, he saw no evidence that anyone was home. His partner should be there shortly. They needed to decide how they would handle what to do next.

A few minutes later, Todd arrived. His partner crouched next to Chase. "Do you think Hammer is in there?"

"I'm not even sure anyone is, but we can't peek in the windows to find out. One of us needs to go up to the cabin and knock."

"It can't be you. He's seen you. I'll do it."

"And I'll go around to the back in case he tries to escape that way."

Todd frowned. "What if he doesn't come to the door?"

"Then we sit out here until we get a warrant or someone returns here."

"Okay. I'll wait until you get around to the back."

At the rear of the cabin, Chase positioned himself behind a large cottonwood then waited. It didn't take long before he spied the blinds being lifted then Hammer raising the window. When the suspect was on the ground, he ran toward the woods in Chase's direction. Perfect. As Hammer neared, Chase stepped out from behind the tree with his gun pointed at Kate's attacker.

Hammer froze.

"Hands up in the air," Chase said as he moved closer.

Hammer did as he was instructed.

After Chase snapped the handcuffs on the suspect's wrist, he stared at the man who probably had threatened Kate and Jamie. Chase's protective instincts rose to the surface. "Let's go to the police station."

"Why?" Hammer pivoted toward Chase. "I haven't done anything wrong."

"We've got some evidence that says otherwise."

"Evidence? From what, my car? It was stolen a few days ago. You should be out there looking for the real criminal."

"Then why didn't you report your car stolen?"

"I know the police. You wouldn't listen to my side of things."

"Tell you what," Chase said, grasping the man's arm and guiding him toward the front of the cabin, "you can tell me your story at the station."

When Chase, Todd and their suspect arrived at the police station, Hammer was arrested and read his rights. Then Hammer demanded a phone to call his lawyer. While Chase waited for the attorney, he and his partner would fill out the paperwork.

Sitting at his desk, Chase called Kate to let her know they found Hammer and he'd been arrested.

When she answered, she asked, "Are you all right?"

"Yes, but I have Hammer sitting in an interrogation room. We'll interview him, but since he lawyered up, he might not talk. Hopefully his lawyer will convince him to cooperate when he is faced with the evidence against him. Afterward, Todd and I are going to the cabin to see what we can find that might help your case."

"Do you want me to tell your brother he doesn't have to stay?"

"Let me interview Hammer and check the cabin before you cut Chad loose. Wait until I get to your house." He also wanted to review the evidence against the suspect.

"See you later. Another Walker has won over my son."

Chase said goodbye then started sorting through what had been gathered against Hammer so far.

Todd stopped by his desk, grinning. "I pushed the lab about processing the ski mask for any hair samples and there are red hairs about the length of Hammer's hair inside it. If he doesn't cooperate, we'll get a court order for a sample from him to see if it matches."

"Good. I'm going to show Kate a photo of the ski mask. It was the same color, but she got a better look than I did. If she can't tell with the picture, we'll do a lineup for her."

"Now that's a first. Ski mask lineup."

"I don't want any doubts that Hammer did it." Chase always tried to do his best but with Kate and Jamie even more so. They were special to him.

After Kate received a call that Chase was on the way to her house, she double-checked the beef stew then hurried upstairs to change. As she stood in her closet reviewing her options of what she could wear, she couldn't make up her mind—casual, a pair of slacks and blouse, or more formal, a soft, silk red dress with a scooped neckline and three-quarter-length sleeves.

She finally picked the dress and donned it. When she viewed herself in the mirror on her closet door, she realized she hadn't dressed up since James died. She ran her hand over the red silk and loved the feel of it against her palm. She didn't want to give the wrong message, but the outfit made her feel feminine, and she hadn't experienced that in a couple of years.

She slipped on the matching red shoes and headed into the hallway. Sounds of two men talking in the foyer floated up to her, and she hurried her pace, looking forward to seeing Chase, safe with Zed Hammer locked up in jail.

When she spotted Chase, her heart skipped a beat. He held a sleepy Jamie in his arms and looked so natural with her son. Jamie had played hard today with Mac and Chad, and although her son had taken a nap, he would go to bed early tonight. He'd never had this much company and action at the house before. Since James's death, she'd lived a quiet and sedate life.

As she descended the stairs, she smiled at that last thought. She certainly didn't condone being attacked and fighting off a kidnapper to add spice to anyone's routine.

Chase caught sight of her and twisted in her direction, his eyes sparkling as he slowly tracked his gaze down her. "I'd give you a wolf whistle, but I wouldn't want to scare Jamie."

"I decided to celebrate Hammer's arrest tonight," she said as her son nestled his head on Chase's shoulder, his eyelids sliding close.

"I'm all for that." Chase's grin slowly encompassed his whole face and reached deep into his eyes.

He drank her in—as though they were totally alone.

Chad cleared his throat. "That's my cue to leave. It sounds like you aren't gonna need me again."

She reached the first floor. "I thought you were going to stay for dinner."

"Your son wore me out. I didn't know a young boy could have so much energy."

Chase laughed. "I was there when you were that age and believe me you could have beaten Jamie. You hardly took a nap most days."

Chad laughed. "I had to keep up with you, bro."

After Chase's brother left, Rachel came into the foyer. Surprise flashed into her eyes at the sight of Kate's fancy dress. "I've got the table set although now I wish I had in the dining room."

Heat flooded Kate's cheeks. "The kitchen is fine."

"I'll take Jamie upstairs and put him to bed. There's a TV show I want to watch, so I'll grab something later." Rachel slid her a small smile. "If I don't see you when you leave, Chase, I want to thank you for being here. I'm thrilled you've caught the man."

"So am I, Rachel." He passed Kate's son to the nanny, Jamie snuggling up against her.

"Good night, hon." Kate kissed Jamie. "I'll check on you later."

While Rachel headed up the stairs with Jamie, Kate turned to Chase.

"So it went well with Hammer?" She started toward the kitchen, starving for food and information about her attacker—and for the chance to get to know Chase better.

"Short of him confessing, we got everything I could have wanted. Todd and I found more evidence to place him at the scene. Today, we discovered the ski mask he used." Chase retrieved his cell phone and showed her several photos of it from different angles. "Is that the type of mask he wore?"

"It looks like it is, but to be sure I would need to see it in person. That was about all I saw when I was struggling with him—that and his dark brown eyes." Kate trembled at the memory of his face thrust close to hers. It had smelled like...cigarettes. "Does Hammer smoke?"

"I saw ashtrays full of butts at the cabin and come to think of it, at his house, too, so I would say yes."

"I can't believe I'd forgotten that was the smell that nauseated me."

After assisting Kate to sit, Chase took the chair cater-corner from her. "Lots of victims forget things and then slowly remember details after the trauma. I've had people forgot almost everything, the event a blur for them. I'll show you the ski mask tomorrow. How about lunch time? I'll pick you up, bring you to the station and set a lineup with black ski masks. Hammer says he doesn't own a ski mask. He gave us a sample of his hair to rule him out. I'll know the results hopefully tomorrow, so until then I'd like to remain here with Mac. That'll be the piece of evidence that will nail the case."

"Not to mention the photos found at his house, his vehicle being the getaway car, his threats against me, his build being the same as my attacker and the fact he tried to escape the police." As she listed the evidence, a peace settled over her. She would have her life back after tomorrow.

He covered her hand on the table between them. "I hope we'll continue to see each other."

"I'd like that very much." Whenever she was in Chase's presence, she was torn between wanting to pull away so she could stay in the safe, isolated world she'd constructed for herself—protected from being vulnerable or getting hurt again—and thinking that it was time to put her life back together and move forward. Could Chase be part of that? She hoped—at least as a friend.

*But what about more?*

Even if the time came when they both were ready to accept that was what they wanted, would it be possible? She remembered their conversation about having children. Children she could never give him.

Warmth spread across her face. She was attracted to the police detective, and she thought he was to her, but that didn't mean getting married. Could she open herself up to the pain she'd experienced when her husband had died? Maybe it would be better to be content to be a mother.

They would never eat if she continued this train of thinking. "We'd better dig in before it gets cold."

"I agree. And let's not talk about the case anymore tonight."

She lifted her glass of tea. "Agreed."

As she passed the food to Chase, she asked, "Chad told me that when your dad left you became the man of the house."

"I was the oldest and Mom needed help. Now she's remarried and has a man who treats her right. My father never hit her, but he put her down all the time. When my dad left, it was like a pall had been lifted from the house."

"Were you the one who taught Chad to play ball?"

"Yes. I never did nearly as well as he did."

"Do you know that he joined the police force because you had?"

Chase plucked a roll out of the bread basket. "He's never told me that, but I figured as much. He used to follow me around everywhere, and when I was with a girl, he would downright embarrass me. But I've gotten him back a few times since he started seeing the receptionist at the station."

Chase described how he'd hung a sign at the baseball field announcing to the crowd that the coach was dating Bailey the first time Chad's girlfriend came to a game. Kate couldn't stop laughing as Chase detailed the many tricks his younger brother had tried to get back at Chase until Chad finally gave up. "I could always top him and a few weeks ago he decided to surrender."

"Are you sure he has?"

"What did he say to you?"

"Nothing, but Chad doesn't seem like the kind of guy to say uncle."

Chase used the roll to clean up the last of the beef stew on his plate. "You know, you're right. No telling what he's planning."

As they cleaned up the dinner dishes, Chase tried to find out everything Chad had asked her. She finally threw up her hands and said, "I can't help you. He never said a word, it's just a gut feeling I have."

"Did he put you up to saying that?"

She chuckled. "No, but obviously he should have tried that. It's working."

Chase put the last plate into the dishwasher. "Yeah, you have a point."

"Maybe let him win one."

"You're probably right. But I always thought the big brother should get the upper hand."

"I can't answer that. I don't have siblings, although listening to you two talk makes me wish I did." She went to the refrigerator and removed a chocolate pie. "Chad told me you love chocolate. Would you like a slice with decaf coffee?"

"Yes to both. I'm going to check the house first."

"Sounds good. I'll bring this into the den. That's where

Mac is. Jamie and Chad wore him out. He's sleeping on the couch."

He moved closer toward her. "If he gets up, I'll put him outside then he can go back to sleep."

"You know, Mac has spoiled us. We're going to have to get a dog. What do you think about getting one from the pound?"

"If you want, I'll go with you. I'm not an expert, but I've had a few in the past. Maybe I can steer you in the right direction."

She turned to look at him, and smiled. "Careful," she teased. "You'll get us used to having *you* around to look out for us, too."

He took another step closer before reaching out to run his fingers through her hair and hook some behind her ear.

She tilted her chin up, leaning her head into his touch. His mouth was inches away. In that moment she wanted him to kiss her. Every fiber of her being screamed for him to.

# SIX

Chase knew he shouldn't, but he couldn't resist Kate's lure. When her beautiful, brown eyes looked into his, he couldn't hold back any longer. He slowly dipped his head toward hers, giving her a chance to pull back.

When she didn't, he grazed his lips over hers so softly he barely touched her. When she leaned in to deepen the contact, he wrapped his arms around her and pressed her against him, releasing his emotions he'd pent up since he'd first heard her screaming for help. The sound still echoed through his mind when he fell asleep.

He needed to rein in his feelings and focus on protecting her. But the effect of their kiss mocked that declaration. He leaned back, staring into her half-closed eyes, a flush tainting her cheeks. He wanted nothing more than to swoop down and kiss her again—and that was exactly why he shouldn't. He needed to stay focused on the goal of making sure she was safe.

He dropped his arms to his side and stepped back. "I'd better check the house and see to Mac."

As he hurried from the kitchen, he tried to tell himself that it was for the best that they had gotten the kiss out of the way so he'd no longer waste time wondering what kissing her would feel like. He now knew and could move on.

*Yeah right, Walker, that's a brilliant suggestion. How are you going to forget that kiss?*

On Monday during her lunch break, Kate assessed the five black ski masks, similar only in color. One was an acrylic knit with wide ribbing while another had ribs that were side by side. There was also a smooth stretchable cotton mask. The logos varied and two didn't have any. The slits for the eyes and mouth were different shapes.

"I didn't realize there were so many different black ski masks." Kate walked the length of the table.

Chase stood on the other side from her. "Neither did I until I went shopping for them. Because of the season, I ended up begging people I knew to let me borrow theirs."

"Can I touch them?"

"Yes."

After looking at each one, she went back down the table and stroked her fingers across the material. Then Kate closed her eyes and tried to recall her struggle with her attacker. She didn't remember any logo, certainly not one of another color. Then she tried to remember the feel of the material when her fingers had touched it. Smooth? Rough?

Her eyes popped open. She knew which one. "That's the mask he wore." She pointed to the second from the end.

"Are you sure?" Chase asked in a neutral tone, no indication if she'd picked Zed Hammer's or not.

"Yes."

"That's Hammer's."

She didn't realize she was holding herself so stiffly until she heard his confirmation and her shoulders sagged. "Good. I feel better knowing he's in jail."

Chase gathered the ski masks into a box. "This was taped for court. I'll send a copy to the DA this afternoon."

Kate nodded. "I'm meeting the DA after work today. She wants to talk to me about the case."

"Are you going to the arraignment tomorrow afternoon?"

"Yes. I asked for it to be at the end of the day so I could attend without cancelling part of my scheduled trials. I'm pushing for no bail. Until his trial, I want him in jail."

"Are you sure about going? You don't have to."

Other than his photo—and the attack—Kate hadn't seen Zed Hammer in a month, since he was in her court. She needed to face him before his trial. It would be easier for her then when she had to testify against the man later. "Yes, I'm sure."

"Then I'll meet you outside the courtroom and sit with you."

"You don't have to."

"I know. But sometimes I do it for some victims, especially when they don't have family nearby. When a person's safety has been threatened, it can change how he looks at life. I just like the injured party to know he has someone on his side."

His offer only confirmed what a caring and honorable man Chase was. That wasn't part of his job, but he did it anyway. "May I ask a favor of you?" Kate said as they left the interview room.

"Of course."

"Come to dinner tonight. Jamie is getting used to you being around. I didn't want you to suddenly no longer be around."

"That's easy. Yes, I will, and I'll make it a point to stop by and see Jamie—and you—after this."

Her son had few men in his life. She shouldn't have been surprised how fast he'd bonded with Chase, but she had been. The whole weekend when Jamie was up, he'd follow Chase or Mac around every chance he got. "I'd like that."

Chase opened the passenger door for Kate then rounded the hood and slipped behind the steering wheel. "Give me a call when you're through with court today. I'll swing by and pick you up. Hopefully I'll have gotten the hair comparison from the ski mask and Hammer's sample we obtained."

On the short drive to the courthouse, Kate leaned back and released a long sigh. "I can't wait until this is over with. I feel like I'm the ball in a juggler's act being constantly tossed up in the air, not sure if I'm going to be caught or not."

He chuckled. "That's an interesting way to put it. I haven't heard that one."

When Chase parked, Kate opened her door. "You don't have to escort me inside. You've got the right man in jail."

He exited the car at the same time she did. "Humor me. I'll feel better when the report on the hair samples come back from the lab with a proven match for Hammer."

Kate took the stairs to the second floor where her office and courtroom were. At the door into her office, she turned toward Chase. "I'll be praying for good results from the lab."

He grasped her hand and stepped nearer. Her heart sped up a bit at his closeness, but all he did was smile at her and say, "I'll see you in a few hours."

As he walked away, she couldn't believe she'd wanted him to kiss her in the corridor of the courthouse and was disappointed he hadn't. She kept repeating that he had a dangerous job, and she didn't ever want to lose someone she loved again the way she had lost James. When Chase wasn't around so much, she was sure she would begin to think logically concerning him.

* * *

"She's expecting you." Kate's assistant waved Chase into her office when he came by later to pick her up.

While lounging against the front of her desk, Kate had her briefcase and purse in hand. She straightened and said, "What were the lab results on the hair samples?"

He grinned. "The hair in the ski mask was Hammer's."

She blew out a long breath. "I knew it, but it's nice to have it confirmed."

"That's exactly how I felt."

"Now all I have to get through is the arraignment tomorrow. If he stays in jail until his trial, I'll feel as though I have my life back."

"But if he doesn't, we'll figure something out. I can always stay at your house."

"I appreciate the offer, but that would mean you'd be on duty twenty-four seven. That's not good for any length of time."

When she passed him strolling toward the door, he caught her arm and halted her. She glanced at him, and he said, "I'll do what is needed and is the best for all involved. I won't let someone be hurt if I can do anything to stop it. My job is to protect, not walk away because I don't get a few hours off."

Her stare drilled into him as though she were trying to figure out the hidden meaning behind his words. "Everyone needs rest, even you."

"I'll be fine. You don't need to worry about me." He left her office, waiting for her in the hallway.

"I'm sure you will, but there's more to life than work. What do you do for fun?" Kate asked as they descended the stairs to the first floor of the courthouse.

"I jog."

When they left the building and hurried to his car, she

said, "I do too, as you know, but I don't classify that as pleasure."

"I enjoy it."

She laughed. "Okay, what else do you enjoy doing?"

Chase didn't answer her question until he started his vehicle and pulled out of the parking lot. He tried to think what else he did in his free time. Not much.

"Surely you do something besides jogging."

"Working," he finally said at a stoplight. "It's not so much that I enjoy it, but I do feel fulfilled by it. In the last skirmish I was involved in while in the Marine Corps, I told you I was shot, but I didn't tell you everything. I would be dead if my partner hadn't covered me. He took a bullet that should have hit me. And when the enemy moved through afterward to make sure they'd gotten us all, I also think his body over mine kept them from checking to see if I was alive."

The light turned green, and he pressed the accelerator, wishing he could escape. He didn't talk about his experience with anyone. Most of the mandatory counseling sessions afterward had consisted of him dancing around the real issue—he'd survived when no one else had in his unit. But he felt the need to share with Kate.

"While you're seeing to others, you still have to take care of yourself. Otherwise you become burnt out."

"I don't want others to feel the helplessness I experienced, trapped there with my friends who I hadn't been able to save. So my job is my way of paying it forward. It took me over four months to recover from my injuries and another three to regain my strength to the point I could re-apply for the police force job I'd had before joining up. The police chief promoted me to detective after three months on the force again. I have a knack for solving cases because I'm determined that the victims get a resolution."

He drove into her driveway, stopped the car and hurried to open his door.

Kate grasped his arm, halting his escape. "And I'm thankful the Lord sent you to me. What I've been going through because of Zed Hammer isn't nearly as bad as it could have been because you were here every step, helping me where you could. There are no words that can adequately describe how I feel about you going above and beyond your job description."

Her hand about him loosened. He quickly slipped from the driver's seat. He suddenly realized he didn't want her gratitude—he was never comfortable with that—but he did want something more personal from her. Confusion flooded him. He cared for her beyond what he would for a victim in a crime he was investigating, and that scared him more than he wanted to acknowledge.

She went ahead of him and opened the front door then looked back at him.

He should leave. She was safe now, but she'd invited him to dinner and Mac and Jamie were inside. He couldn't escape that easily, and there was a part of him that didn't want to. Until he'd met her, he'd been focused on what he felt his mission was, to protect others. Now she was challenging it.

When he stepped into the foyer, Jamie spied him and ran as fast as he could and threw his arms around Chase's legs. "Case, home."

Emotions jammed Chase's throat. He bent over and picked the little boy up. Holding him felt so right. If the only thing Kate felt for him was gratitude, then why had she kissed him? He didn't have an answer, but he knew it wasn't enough to base a relationship on.

Late the next afternoon, Kate sat next to Chase in the courtroom at Zed Hammer's arraignment, gripping Chase's hand as the DA asked for no bail, basing the request on the nature of the crime against a child and the possible flight risk.

When Hammer's lawyer stood and objected, Kate held her breath. Her lungs burned, and she finally had to blow out a soft sigh. The attorney took his seat while his client glanced at her. Hammer's look, filled with hatred, chilled her to the marrow of her bones. She tensed.

Chase leaned close and whispered into her ear, "Don't let him get to you."

When the judge announced his decision about the bail— five hundred thousand dollars, an amount that she was certain Hammer couldn't afford—relief melted the tension gripping her as tight as she was Chase's hand.

Zed Hammer exploded, leaping to his feet. "I didn't do anything wrong. The police are framing me because of her." He jabbed his finger in the air at her. "I don't own a ski mask and my car was stolen."

The judge rapped his gavel repeatedly through Zed Hammer's last words. The defense lawyer yanked his client down into his chair as the bailiff closed in on the defendant.

Chase rose and pulled her to her feet. "Let's get out of here."

In the hallway, Kate was still trying to process the scene in the courtroom. The hatred she'd seen in Zed Hammer's eyes wrapped around her and squeezed, making it hard to draw in a decent breath. Her heartbeat raced so fast she felt lightheaded.

Chase found a nearby alcove that was private and vacant. He drew her against him and his arms went around her. She concentrated on the feel, a cocoon of safety and support.

"We know the case is a good one and so does the judge,

or he wouldn't have set such a high bail. Hammer is trying to play a head game with you. Don't let him. He'll have his say in court, but in the meantime you'll be able to go through your day without worrying where the man is. I'm not letting anything happen to you or Jamie."

*I can't go through losing Jamie. He's innocent.*

"Kate?"

Chase's voice penetrated her momentary panic from the scene in the courtroom. She pulled back. "I'm okay. I've been holding myself together for five days and I just lost it for a moment. I was fine last night. It was his look that got to me."

Chase clasped her upper arms. "That's what he was going for, but tonight he's the one who will still be in jail. Let's go. I'll walk you to your car then follow you to your house."

"You don't have to do that. Really. I'm all right."

"Okay, but will you promise me to call at any time if you need someone to talk to?"

She nodded and headed for the staircase to the first floor. "Yes. You can't get rid of me that easily."

Though they hadn't known each other for long, they had developed a camaraderie that went beyond friendship. The conversation they'd had yesterday on the way to her house highlighted that. The only man she'd ever talked like that with was James. Maybe in time, when this case was over, they could have a long discussion about where they might be heading. But right now, she needed to remain focused on the upcoming trial and on protecting herself and her son from someone like Zed Hammer.

At her car, Chase opened the door for her. When she sat behind the steering wheel, he leaned in. "I think Mac is having withdrawal symptoms with Jamie not being around. Can we plan something this weekend? Maybe go to the park."

"Jamie would love that. So would I." The prospect lifted

her spirits. The past five days had been so intense. How-ever, she didn't want to not see Chase—or Mac. "I'll talk to you in a day or so."

He pushed away from the car and watched as she drove out of the parking lot. She'd missed him and Mac last night more than she should have. This morning when Chase and his dog weren't at the house, Jamie hadn't understood why not.

When she walked in the front door, Jamie looked behind her, no doubt for Chase and Mac. "Case? Mac?"

"They're at their home, but we'll see them in a few days."

A pout formed on Jamie's face. "No. Now."

She picked up her son and held him close. "Soon, hon."

The rest of the evening was spent trying to take Jamie's mind off the missing duo. She definitely needed to see about getting a dog for her son as soon as possible. That might help him adjust to them not being around all the time.

After he was asleep, she went to her room and collapsed on the bed, staring at the ceiling. How was *she* going to adjust to Chase not being around? She might have it worse than Jamie.

Exhaustion set in and slowly her eyes grew heavier until sleep whisked her away. She surrendered to the darkness, floating, relaxing…

Something jerked her wide awake. She sat up straight, staring into the blackness.

Suddenly she jumped out of her bed, fumbled with her lamp and switched it on. She scanned the room. Nothing had changed.

She headed out into the hallway. Still nothing. Then her gaze latched onto her son's bedroom, and she quietly eased the door open, the soft illumination of the nightlight allowing her to see that…

Jamie was gone!

# SEVEN

"Jamie, where are you?"

Nothing.

Trying to remain calm, Kate switched on the overhead light. In the middle of her son's bedroom, Kate turned in a full circle, hoping he'd climbed out of bed and was playing a hide-and-seek game with her. Her chest constricted so tightly that she could hardly breathe. The beating of her heart thundered against her skull, and her sweaty hands shook. He was nowhere.

*Help, Lord.*

She stared out into the hall. Jamie couldn't open the door because the knob was too hard for him to turn—at least so far. Even if he had opened it, he wouldn't have shut it.

What if he'd awakened crying and Rachel had taken Jamie to her room to calm him down? She'd done that a couple of times in the past when he was upset.

She rushed into the corridor and ran to Rachel's bedroom and pounded on the door.

Rachel swung her door open, her hair messy, her eyes half-closed. "What's wrong?"

"Is Jamie in your room?"

"No, why?"

"Jamie isn't in his bed or room. Start at this end of the hall and check everywhere a small child could hide." Kate would take the other end.

As she passed the steps with the gate across it, she held her breath as she looked down the staircase. He was starting to climb more so she needed to consider the option that he might have climbed over the gate. But there was no sign of Jamie on the stairs or at the bottom.

While Rachel called out her son's name several times, Kate did likewise when she entered each room. With each step she took without finding her son, her heartbeat kicked up a notch.

When she met Rachel in the center of the hallway, Kate dragged air into her lungs. Panic began to set in, and she tried to remain as calm as she could but it was impossible. If she fell apart, she wouldn't be able to help find her son.

"Kate, did you go upstairs to the attic?"

"No, why?"

Rachel gestured at the attic door nearby. "I didn't either, but the door is ajar."

Kate pivoted toward it and moved closer, noticing for the first time it hadn't been shut all the way. It was always closed tightly and locked because of Jamie. *Someone had been in her home.*

Sweat beaded her upper lip and forehead. "Check downstairs just in case. I'm calling Chase." She couldn't deny it any longer. Someone had taken Jamie.

"You aren't going up in the attic by yourself, are you?"

"I am, after I load my husband's handgun. I don't know how anyone could get into the attic without setting off the alarm. Check and make sure it's working."

Rachel hurried down the stairs, glanced at the security pad and said, "It's still on."

Kate went to the gun safe in her bedroom and retrieved

the pistol, along with the ammo in the closet. James had made her take lessons on handling it. She hadn't even wanted one in the house, but when he was traveling, he'd felt better if she had it nearby.

For the first time she loaded it with the purpose of using it if she had to. Then she grabbed her cell phone and called Chase as she headed for the attic.

When he answered, his voice sounded as though he'd been in a deep sleep.

With no time to waste, Kate launched into her spiel. "Jamie is gone. I can't find him anywhere."

"I'll be there in ten minutes. I'll call headquarters."

"I'll tell Rachel to let you in. I'm going up in the attic to check."

"The attic? Why?"

"The door was slightly open. It never is."

"Can you shut the door and lock it so it can't be opened from the inside?"

"Yes."

"Do that, then get downstairs. Do not go into the attic. I'm getting into my car. I'll be there in a few minutes." He hung up.

Kate approached the entrance to the attic. With her hands shaking, she carefully closed the door and secured it as Chase had instructed. That was when she realized, it should have already been locked. Panic was scrambling her thought processes.

*Lord, please help me to remain calm. I can't do this without You.*

She backed away, ready to lift her gun if someone burst through the attic door. How did anyone get up there?

At the staircase, she threw one last glance down the hall then descended the steps so fast she nearly stumbled. She grabbed the banister and slowed her pace.

Not only was she thinking irrationally, but she was risking sending herself to the hospital with a broken bone.

She planted herself at the window that afforded her a good view of the porch and front door. The second she saw Chase's car come to a screeching halt, she ran into the foyer and turned off the alarm then stood in the main entrance as he jogged to her house.

The sight of him calmed her frazzled nerves for a few seconds. Chase knew what to do. At least she wasn't alone to handle the situation.

He embraced her. "Todd is coming and a couple of other police officers." He moved into the entry hall, his arm along her shoulders. "Rachel, I'd appreciate it if you'd wait here for the others to arrive. Tell my partner we'll be upstairs. I'm going to check out the attic."

As Kate mounted the stairs with Chase beside her, she reached for his hand and clasped it. The physical and emotional connection between them fortified Kate with each step closer to the attic. "You think someone got in through the attic and took Jamie? How?"

"I don't know. It's three stories up. No windows. But if the door to it was open, something—or someone—caused it. The answer might be up there." He pointed at the ceiling.

"Let's go." She pulled the key from her pocket.

After he unlocked the door, he peered back at her. "Stay here."

"No."

Both of his eyebrows hiked up.

"I'll follow at a distance, but I'm going. This is my son, my house." *God is with me.*

"Okay. Wait until I get to the top of the stairs and scan the area."

Kate kept her gaze trained on Chase as he ascended. The musty, dusty air tickled her nose and caused her to sneeze. Her allergies were the reason she rarely went to the third story. But if it would help her find her son, she didn't care. She'd camp out up there if it meant Jamie was all right and safe.

Chase waved her up the stairs. She hurried up them, sneezing again.

"When was the last time you were up here?" he asked as he moved away from the steps. Although two overhead lights illuminated the large open space, he withdrew a small but powerful flashlight and shined it in places between boxes and pieces of old furniture.

"Right after James died. He was the one who dealt with getting things in and out of the attic." Another sneeze accompanied her words. "Now you see why."

"Go back downstairs. I can check this out alone."

"No, I'll take the other side." She focused on the task at hand and covered her nose with her cupped hand to stifle the sound of her overactive allergy to dust.

As she searched behind an old dresser, Chase said, "I think I know how someone might have gotten in."

She spun around and spied him standing at the far end. Behind him was a louvered gable vent. "How?"

"This type of vent opens. It would be a tight fit, but a man could get in this way." Chase put latex gloves on and pushed on a door that swung away from the house. "I'm checking the one at the other end. Then I'll go outside and see what is below them. But this is a possible way into your attic, therefore your house."

"I'm sure the door up to this floor was locked."

"A lock can be picked."

"And that door was never wired into the alarm system."

"Nor your gable vents."

She sneezed again.

"Go downstairs and let Todd know. I'll be there shortly."

When Kate returned to the second floor, Todd emerged from one of the spare bedrooms. "Chase found a way someone could have gotten inside the attic." She told his partner about the gable vents.

Todd started for the attic door, but Chase came out into the hallway. "I'll check the left side of the house. I need you to search the right, especially under the vent," he instructed his partner. "Where are the other officers?"

"Going through the ground floor." Todd headed toward the staircase.

"Post them at the front and back doors." Chase stopped in front of Kate. "When was the last time you saw Jamie?"

"I always check on him before I go to bed. That was eleven."

"Whoever came into your house did between eleven and two."

"So you believe my son has been kidnapped?" she asked, even though she already knew the answer.

Chase nodded.

"Why didn't I hear anything?"

"The kidnapper was probably careful to make as little noise as possible. Your bedroom and Rachel's are on the right side of the house. I think he used the left gable vent. It would be harder for you to hear anything going on outside and above you."

But had she heard something? Was that why she woke up so suddenly?

Chase paused at the top of the steps. "Are you coming downstairs?"

She had to be strong for Jamie. Falling apart wouldn't help her son. "No, I'll be in Jamie's room."

"Don't touch anything. The kidnapper probably wore gloves, but in case he didn't, we'll be taking latent prints."

He moved in her direction, as if he'd changed his mind about investigating outside.

She held up her palm. "I'm not going to mess up the crime scene. I…" Her throat closed around the words she'd wanted to say. She swallowed several times.

He took another step.

"I—I need to be alone. Please just find my son." Tears flooded her eyes.

As he came closer, all she saw was a blur. Then she felt his strong arms encase her in a protective shield, and she clung to him for a few seconds while she willed her sorrow to the dark recesses of her mind. There was no time for this distress. It could immobilize her. Finally, she pushed away from him, swiped the wetness from her cheeks and turned to go into her son's room.

She stood in the middle of it, not looking back to see if Chase was there. If she did, she'd come unglued. She needed to think rationally, like she did every day on the job. Assess the evidence. Dig into her past cases. Find this person who took Jamie and get her son back.

*Lord, if I have to trade myself for Jamie, I will. I'll do anything. Just keep him safe.*

Did Jamie get to take his teddy bear he always held when he went to sleep?

In her frantic search of the room, she couldn't remember if it was in his crib. She closed the space between her and her son's bed. She peeked over the railing. Her gaze fell on Jamie's favorite stuffed animal, Bobo. He would be totally alone. A dull ache grew in her chest, making it difficult to breathe.

*No, the Lord is with him.*

She picked up the bear and hugged it against her, tears spilling from her eyes. Through the watery sheen, she glimpsed a cell phone where the stuffed animal had been.

She started to touch it and realized she didn't have any gloves on.

What if the kidnapper accidentally lost his phone?

Instead, she took the edge of Jamie's blanket and punched the button to turn it on. The screen lit up with a message to *her*. "If you want your son back, take this phone. Don't tell anyone." At the end was an icon of a tiny skull.

Kate heard footsteps coming toward the room and quickly used the blanket to stuff the phone into her sweatpants' pocket.

Chase appeared in the entrance, took one look at her and crossed to her. "I'm going to do everything I can to find who did this. I have a crime scene team coming. They should be here soon."

"What did you find outside?"

"Under the left side gable vent the ground has been disturbed. Your sprinkle system must have come on because I found a good tennis shoe print. Wide and about size eleven. I also discovered the ladder he used—it was behind the bushes. It looks new. We might be able to find out where it was bought."

He was trying to give her hope. And that was one of the things she loved about him. Should she say anything to him about the phone? If the guy found out, he might disappear with Jamie or...

*Kill him.*

"We need to dig into your cases again, even go back to the beginning when you started as a judge in family court." Chase slung his arm over her shoulders. "Let's go downstairs and let the crime scene techs process this room and the attic. Rachel put on a pot of coffee. I could use some. How about you?"

"I don't think I need coffee to stay awake. I couldn't sleep if I wanted to."

"I'm going to need you to help me with your past trials."

Kate turned toward him. "What if Zed Hammer didn't try to kidnap Jamie before? What if that attacker in the park is the same man who did this tonight?"

"There is a lot of evidence against Hammer. We might be looking at two people working together or separately. Hammer's in jail right now, and that's where he should stay until we figure out what's going on."

"We?"

"Yes, you and I. You know about your trials. I still have that list we made before Hammer was captured. Let's go downstairs and take a look at it."

"You go ahead. I'll be downstairs in a few minutes. I'd like to change clothes. I might as well get dressed for the day."

He cupped the side of her face, such concern in his eyes. "I can wait up here for you."

The strong urge to cling to him and never let him go swamped her. She wanted to tell him about the phone, but the possible consequences of that action were too steep for her. She couldn't risk her child. She needed to think. "I just need a little time to myself. I won't be long."

When Kate disappeared into her bedroom and shut the door, she collapsed against it and sank to the floor.

*Lord, why? Not my baby.*

She finally released the tears she'd been fighting to hold back. They flowed down her cheeks and wet her shirt. She was trying to be strong, but at the moment she felt anything but. She wanted her son back. If she had to risk herself, she would.

Finally, after she reined in her emotions, she slid the cell phone out of her pocket and called the number she'd been given on the screen. There was the click of the call connecting, then silence. Finally she said, "This is Kate Forster."

"Are you alone?" a gruff, bass voice asked.

"Yes."

"The police are at your house. You're not alone."

Kate sat up straight and scanned her bedroom as though the kidnapper was still in her house. "I'd already called them before I found the phone in Jamie's bed. They don't know anything about it."

"You're going to give me something—and when you do, if I see one cop around, you'll never see your son again."

She didn't want to think about that option. "What's the ransom?" If she had to sell everything she had, she would to raise the money.

He chuckled. "Really pretty easy and cheap. I want to know where Janice Holifield and her two sons are—plus a hundred thousand dollars."

The money wouldn't be a problem, but Janice Holifield? The name sounded so familiar, but she couldn't place why at the moment. How could she supply the location of this woman and children even if she remembered where they lived? "Why do you want that address?"

"None of your business. I'll give you twelve hours to come up with the address and money. If I don't hear from you, you'll never see Jamie again."

Before she could say another word, he disconnected the call.

Had Janice Holifield been tied up in a case in her courtroom? That had to be it. Usually those involved a family member, often the spouse. Was that who she'd talked to? Janice's ex-husband?

She glanced at her watch. She had to call him before three o'clock this afternoon.

After shoving herself to her feet, she hurried to her

closet and snatched the first outfit she saw and dressed. She had to find out about Janice Holifield. The woman was probably part of one of her older trials. A faint image of a brown-haired woman came to mind. Was that Janice or someone else?

When she entered the kitchen, the scent of coffee infused the air and drove back any thoughts of sleep. Not that she would be able to rest until Jamie was returned to her.

Chase sat at her table with a big mug next to a stack of physical files she kept on her cases with personal notes and impressions. Rachel drank her coffee, staring into space, a stunned look on her face.

Kate filled her cup and moved to them. "Rachel, try to get some rest. There isn't anything you can do right now."

"But…" The nanny lifted her head, her eyes glittering with tears. "I want to help find Jamie."

"Later. We'll need breakfast and more coffee in a couple of hours. Lie down and rest until then. I have to be the one who goes through each of the cases that came before my court."

After Rachel left, Chase glanced up. "There are a lot of cases here. How should we do this?"

Kate sat. "I'll start from the beginning. You can go from the most recent one and back. Look for any cases where the man was portrayed as violent or dangerous. At least we know it wasn't Zed Hammer tonight. That's one case."

"Out of hundreds. But there's still a chance Hammer has an accomplice. Time is important. I asked Todd to help after the crime scene is processed. If we had a name or something specific to search we could use your computer at work with its database."

*Tell him.* Then she remembered her conversation with the kidnapper. Jamie's life was at stake. Surely she could find that name in her physical files.

"Hopefully as I look through the files, I'll remember incidents that might raise suspicions." Kate snagged the stack of files from eight years before when she first became a family court judge.

She delved into the first case then the next one. An hour later and another cup of coffee, she'd completed half of the trials from the year she'd begun. She stood and stretched then walked to the stove to refill her mug. Even knowing a name connected to her kidnapper, she wasn't going as fast as she thought she would. It was hard to contain her frustration.

"Find anything?" Chase asked as he joined her and topped off his drink.

*Tell him. Put your trust totally in the Lord to protect Jamie. You have less than eleven hours to find this Janice Holifield.*

"Nothing."

"Not even one case we should delve into deeper?"

She shook her head then hastened back to the kitchen table. She couldn't shake the image of a bomb ticking down that would explode at three o'clock.

By the time Rachel made breakfast at six, Kate had almost completed her second year as a judge. Panic seeded itself in her heart and grew.

*Trust in God.*

As she ate her omelet and nibbled on a piece of toast, she finished that stack and moved on to the third year. At a few minutes after seven, she looked up and locked gazes with Chase.

*Tell him.*

Eight hours left and not a mention of a Janice Holifield in her files. And yet the name taunted her. Maybe she missed the reference in her rush?

"What's wrong?" Chase asked, his eyes darkening.

*I can't do this alone.*

She reached into her pocket and withdrew the cell phone from the kidnapper. "We need to search for Janice Holifield."

As Kate explained what happened hours ago and that the kidnapper knew she'd contacted the police, Chase, with latex gloves on, held the cell phone that Kate had slid across to him. He stared at the kidnapper's message to her. He should be upset at her for holding back information, but how could he when he looked at the fear in her expression or heard the catch in her voice?

"I'm sorry I didn't tell you earlier. I thought I would easily find the trial with Janice Holifield and take care of getting Jamie back by myself. I can't lose Jamie, and the kidnapper said that if I told anyone, I'd never see my son again."

He reached across the table and covered her hand. "I know Jamie's special. I'm not going to let you lose him. Yes, it would have been better to know when you found the phone, but I'll get Todd in here to see what he can find out about this Janice Holifield while we look for that name in your files together. I've done two years and you nearly three. We only have three more to go, and now I can go faster. Then once we find her, we can set up something ahead to trap the kidnapper."

"How can you guarantee he won't hurt Jamie?"

"I can't, but I've worked on kidnappings before and I have a good success rate. Will you be able to get the money?"

"Yes, now that the bank is open. I don't know what the rules are for withdrawing that much cash, but I know the bank's president. He'll find a way."

"Good. I'm sending the other police officers away. Todd

can work from the station." Chase stood and moved around
to her, pulling her to her feet and gathering her against him.
"You have a strong faith. Lean on it right now. Believe the
Lord will bring Jamie back to you unhurt by the end of
today." He couldn't tell her that he was disappointed she
hadn't believed in him enough to know he would never
endanger Jamie. Right now her child's safety was the only
thing they should focus on.

"You're right, and I'm trying. When it's something so
important to me, it's hard to turn it over totally to the
Lord."

"Sometimes that's all we can do. That day of the ambush I'd wanted to live and return home. But we all wanted
that, and I was the only one who got it. I still don't understand why I survived and no one else did." He felt such a
weight on his shoulders. He didn't feel worthy to live when
all his buddies didn't.

"God has plans for you." She rose up on tiptoes and
kissed him on his cheek. "Let's get back to work."

"Agreed." As he sat, his cheek tingled where her lips
had touched it.

After he explained everything to Todd, Chase began
skimming the records for Janice Holifield or any Holifield.
He went quickly back through the ones he'd already done,
just in case he'd missed something.

When Kate paused and reread the same page twice,
Chase asked, "Have you found Janice?"

She looked up and nodded.

He rose and rounded the end of the table to peer over
her shoulder at the file. "Do you remember this trial?"

"Yeah, now. I should have before. Janice's husband,
Don, abused his wife and kids. At the divorce hearing, the
wife finally had the strength to testify against her husband
with the help from a counselor she'd met at the Riverside

Women's Shelter. Medical records and neighbors' testimony backed up what Janice said. Don's parental rights were denied. The wife received the bulk of their possessions, and later Don Holifield was convicted in criminal court for the abuse to his wife and children and sent to prison. I didn't realize he was out."

"Did he threaten you?"

She thought for a long moment. "Not exactly. He didn't say anything. He sat silently through the trial. When I gave my verdict, all he did was stare at me with cold eyes. Never a word, though."

"Maybe we can track his whereabouts. Narrow down where he might be." He pulled out his cell phone. "I'm calling Todd to see what he's discovered about any Janice Holifield here in town." When his partner answered, Chase asked, "What do you have?"

"Janice Holifield isn't here in Cimarron City. She moved four years ago and didn't leave any forwarding address."

"Check with her neighbors. Maybe one of them knows where she went. Also the Riverside Women's Shelter where she stayed until her husband was prosecuted." Men who abused women and children should stay in jail much longer than Janice's husband did, and when Chase caught up with this guy, he'd make sure Don did go away for longer.

"I'll let you know if I have any leads by two-thirty."

"Remember, all of this has to be done quietly. Don Holifield can't get wind of this." By the time Chase finished his conversation with his partner, Kate had taken her seat again. Chase sat next to her, one hand on the back of her chair. "Why does he think you can find her address?"

"Janice wrote me at the courthouse three times, although I couldn't correspond with her because it's unethical. Maybe Don found out or Janice told him she was writing to me to make it seem she had a personal relationship with me. She took her maiden name Baker and changed her first name to Trish. She was putting her life back together. The last letter I got from her was right after she married a man who was great to her children and her. He was a minister and was moving to a new church. She didn't want any reminders of her past life so she told me that would be her last letter. I don't know her married name nor where she went. There was so much hope in that message that I immediately felt that Trish—I mean Janice—found what she'd been searching for. I don't always find out a woman is able to put her life back together."

"Do you remember the old address? Someone in that town could know where she went. Maybe we could find a reference online to a local pastor marrying and moving to another church."

"And do what with the information? You can't think that I would tell her ex-husband where she and her children live." Kate scrambled from her seat and stood a few feet away, her arms crossed over her chest. "I want my son back, but there has to be another way without putting an innocent family at risk. Even if it tears me apart to think that Jamie is in the hands of a maniac who abused his own children." Her legs buckled, and she sank toward the floor.

Chase leaped forward and grabbed her before she hit the tiles. His arms enveloped her, and he supported her against him. "I'll find a way. I don't want him to know where his family is, either. They've been terrorized enough, but I want to be able to warn them if I have to."

"Her old address was in my notes on the trial. 5793 Highland Park in Lexington."

"Which state?"

She mumbled the name against his shirt.

"You need to lie down."

"I can't sleep."

"I understand, but you need to rest as much as you can while Todd and I come up with a plan for the exchange." Chase led her into the den where he sat her on the couch. "I won't be far away. If he calls early, I'll get the phone to you."

Chase walked to the exit and looked back. As Kate stretched out on the couch, all he wanted to do was go back and hold her, try to take her pain away. A missing child had to be a parent's worst nightmare.

Hands clamped around her steering wheel shortly after four that afternoon, Kate followed the last set of instructions the kidnapper had phoned her. Chase was in her trunk with a listening device connected to a microphone in the car so he could pick up what she was saying.

"I'm a block away from Lynn Lane and Buffalo," she said as loud as she could without moving her lips. She had no idea how the kidnapper knew exactly where she was, but in case he had eyes on her, she didn't want it to be apparent that she was letting anyone know where she was going.

This area of Cimarron City had quite a few older structures, some deserted. Which one was the man in? Or would he send her somewhere else? She'd spent the last hour traveling from one obscure part of town to another.

The phone rang again. She punched the accept button.

"Park behind the redbrick building next to the abandoned warehouse in the back. Then get out and walk south toward the field. Hurry. You have a minute to get to the back of the parking lot where the field is. Bring the money. No cell phone."

She turned off the engine, quickly leaned over so no one could see her talk and grabbed the duffel bag with the one thousand one-hundred-dollar bills. "I have a minute to get to the field. I have to leave my cell phone."

Then she clambered out of her car and jogged toward

the high weeds and grass behind the warehouse. Was the kidnapper hiding in there? Did he have Jamie with him?

The sound of a motorcycle in the pasture coming toward her slowed her step. The wall of green parted as a tall, thin man in a black biker helmet raced toward her. She froze.

He skidded to an abrupt stop and thrust a black helmet into her chest. "Give me the money and put this on."

She did as she was told. The last thing she saw before slipping the helmet on was him dumping the money into a compartment on his bike.

He gripped her hand and yanked her toward him. "Get on. We're leaving."

"Where's Jamie?" She couldn't see anything. The shield over her face was totally darkened as if he'd painted it black.

"Not here."

She wanted to scream, "I know. Where?" But she kept those thoughts to herself.

She didn't want to put her arms around him, so she grasped the sides of the seat the best she could. He revved the engine, and the motorcycle jumped forward. Kate jerked back and nearly flew off the bike. She dug her fingernails into the leather and hung on.

"Brace yourself," the kidnapper said through the intercom system in the helmets.

The next thing she heard and felt was the blast of a nearby explosion. What had blown up, and why? Her answer came a moment later, punctuated with the kidnapper's cackles. "You didn't need that car." The sound of his voice reverberated through her.

The meaning of what he said ping-ponged through her mind. Chase had been in the trunk.

*He's dead!*

# EIGHT

*Chase died protecting Jamie and me.*

*Why, Lord? He is—was—a good man. I cared for him.*

She'd tried to protect herself against having this wrenching sorrow flood her but it had happened anyway. And despite the pain she now felt, she couldn't regret the time she'd had with Chase, even though it had been far too short. Tears streamed down her cheeks. She was going to survive, get her son back and somehow make sure that Don Holifield went to jail for the rest of his life.

*That's all I can do for Chase now.* Emotions crammed her throat as the motorcycle turned sharply to the right. The terrain turned bumpy. The slap of the tall weeds and grass against her legs hardly registered as Don Holifield plowed through the field behind the warehouse.

The bike came to a sudden halt, and she fell from the motorcycle, skidding over rocky ground. She momentarily thought about trying to escape, but that wouldn't get her son back.

Instead she removed the helmet, blinking from the bright sunlight filtering through the trees overhead, while Don Holifield stood over her. She lifted her gaze to his dark eyes boring into her. The urge to squirm was strong, but she refused to give him the satisfaction of seeing the fear that held her. She focused instead on his shaved head.

"I have my ransom money. What's the address for my wife and kids?"

She ground her teeth together and pushed herself to her feet. He still had a height advantage, but now, she got a good look at her surroundings. Glimpses of the lake through the woods gave her an idea of where she was. She didn't recognize the setting, but she saw a shack nestled in overgrown brush to the left. Was Jamie inside?

She tilted her chin up and stared into his dark snake eyes. "Not until I see that my son is okay."

He assessed her with razor-sharp precision. She didn't look away.

"He's in the shack."

She held her ground, clutching the helmet. She'd use it as a weapon if she had to, but she knew it wasn't a match for the gun stuck in his waistband. "I need to see him first."

He took a stepped closer, and she stiffened, preparing herself for his blow.

"You aren't calling the shots here. This isn't your court-room."

With lightning-quick reflexes, the kidnapper reached for her, his big hands going around her neck. He squeezed, closing off her throat.

The explosion slammed Chase to the parking lot pave-ment, the impact knocking the air from his lungs. He'd used the emergency lever to get out of the trunk after Kate had exited, but he hadn't moved very far, meaning he'd been only about a hundred yards away when the car ex-ploded. His ears rang as he rolled over, struggled to sit up and stared at what used to be Kate's car. His cell phone vibrated in his pocket. Chase quickly retrieved it and saw it was Todd calling.

Chase answered. "The kidnapper set off a bomb in Kate's car. I can't hear well, but I'm at Lynn Lane and Buffalo. Hurry. Call the fire department."

He scanned the area. He'd heard a motorcycle earlier. The kidnapper must have been riding it. It was gone now with no one left behind, so he had probably taken Kate with him, but which way did he go?

He pulled up the tracking program that was tied to a necklace he'd given Kate before she headed out to meet Don Holifield.

Chase fixed his gaze on the blinking red dot on the screen and breathed easier. He tried to stand, wobbled and sank back down. He didn't have time to be off balance. He had to find Kate and Jamie.

While he attempted to stand a second time, Todd's SUV came barreling around the corner of the warehouse and headed straight for Chase. This time he managed to stay upright. His ears still rang, but the noise wasn't as loud as it had been ten minutes ago.

His partner parked next to Chase, and he hurriedly slipped into Todd's passenger seat. "I've got her signal." He hoped. It was stationary right now. He prayed that was because she was with her son, not because Holifield had made her get rid of her jewelry—or killed her.

Chase directed his partner to go to the left while two patrol cars and a fire truck sped across the parking lot, their sirens off.

"Did he know you were in the trunk?" Todd asked.

"I don't think so. What I want to know is where the bomb came from. Her car has been kept in the garage since the first attack—except today. It was parked in the lot behind the courthouse." Chase pointed to the field on the left. "You need to turn here. The tracker indicates she's not far from the south end of the lake."

"Is she moving or stationary?"

"She hasn't gone anywhere in the past five minutes." Chase didn't have a good feeling about this, but he didn't voice his concerns. Kate's only objective was rescuing Jamie, but returning the child might never have been Holifield's intention.

"Can't tell you if you choke me," Kate managed to get out before the kidnapper's hands cut off her breathing completely.

*Fight!*

*Can't give in.*

Kate clamped her hands around his wrists and tried to yank them away.

Suddenly he released her and slapped her across the face, shoving her away from him. She went down, sucking in air for her oxygen-deprived lungs. He moved toward her. As she scrambled to her feet, she grabbed a handful of dirt and threw it into his face.

He staggered and rubbed his eyes.

Kate landed a few kicks then ran toward the shack. Jamie had to be inside. If not...

She reached the door to the shack, pushing it open. As she crossed the threshold, the kidnapper tackled her to the wooden floor. She pummeled him as she tried to see if Jamie was in the one-room cabin.

Her gaze landed on her baby lying still on his blanket from his crib.

Don Holifield pinned her flinging arms to her side and

thrust his face into hers, his eyes red from the dirt. "You've seen your son. What's the address?"

"I need to make sure he's alive."

"No, you don't, or I'll kill him in front of you."

"I'll give you the address but not the town until I can hold him."

A nerve twitched in his jaw. "Okay."

"5793 Highland Park."

Instead of releasing her, the kidnapper struck her again. She tasted blood in her mouth, and the shack spun.

"You're lying. I know about that address. They're gone from there. Don't play me for a fool. If you don't tell me the real address, I'll kill you both."

She blinked, trying to focus on his face looming over hers. Every deep line of his expression shouted rage. "I don't know any other address."

"Liar." He put his hands around her neck again. *I'm going to die,* she thought. But then a voice that Kate thought she would never hear again filled the shack.

"Get up. Now."

The kidnapper glanced over his shoulder, but Don Holifield didn't move, except to squeeze Kate's throat tighter. A choking sound came from her. His thumbs pressed down.

Then suddenly the man was hauled off her chest, his fingers slipping from her. Air rushed into her aching throat. As she sucked in more, she scooted backward, her gaze fixed on Chase punching the kidnapper. Todd stood to the side with his gun in his hand.

*Jamie!*

Kate turned from the fight and scrambled forward, scooping Jamie against her. He was warm. He was breathing. She sagged in relief as she cuddled her baby against her chest. Tears ran down her face when Chase came to her and helped her to her feet. While Todd put handcuffs on the kidnapper, Chase's arms enfolded her.

"Is Jamie okay?"

She nodded. "I think so. I need to have him checked by a doctor." Her voice cracked, her throat aching.

"You, too," Chase murmured against her hair.

"Take my car," Todd said. "I'll stay with Holifield until backup comes."

"Thanks, Todd." Chase nestled her against his side while she clung to Jamie. Todd tossed him his keys.

A gentle breeze caressed her tearstained cheeks. Her son was alive. So was she. Her attacker was under arrest, and her nightmare was over. Thanks to Chase. *Thank You, Lord.*

Later that night, Chase approached Kate's house, exhausted but needing to see Kate and Jamie before he went home. Earlier, he hadn't left the hospital until he made sure they were both okay.

He'd stood by her side while the doctor examined Jamie and was as relieved as any parent when the pediatrician had told her that her son had been given something to make him sleep but he would be all right.

Then Chase had gone to the police station to personally make sure that the case was wrapped up. Todd could have handled it, but both he and Kate needed to know the details of what had gone down and Hammer's part in everything that happened in the past week.

The front door opened before he had a chance to ring the bell. Kate, standing in the doorway with her bruises starting to show and a couple of small bandages over her cuts, was the best picture he'd ever seen. Without a word, he scooped her into his embrace and just held her against him.

When she leaned back and tilted her chin so she could stare at him, he bent forward and kissed her.

"Is Jamie up?" he whispered against her lips, wanting to kiss her again and never let her go. He'd almost lost her—and Jamie—today.

"Not now. He was up until an hour ago." She caressed the side of his face. "Is it over?" she finally asked as she stepped back to let him inside.

"Yes. With a confession from Holifield, I can say that with confidence." He walked toward the den. "He set up Zed Hammer for the kidnapping attempt in the park, using his car, planting his hair in the ski mask. If the first time had worked and he took Jamie, then that would be great, but if it failed, he wanted someone else who threatened you to take the fall while he planned another attempt."

Kate settled on the couch, tired circles under her eyes. "I get it that he was angry at me for taking away custody of his children and helping his family escape his brutality, but that was almost five years ago."

"He had a lot of time to think about getting revenge on you and his wife. He'd tracked her to the house in Lexington but couldn't find any clues to her location beyond that. He'd known she was corresponding with you when he called her once begging to see his kids before going to prison. She told him she would report it to you, that she wasn't alone anymore. Your decision gave her a glimpse of hope in a bleak situation."

"How did he blow up my car? It was in the garage except for yesterday. Did he get to it and plant it then before taking Jamie? Or in the parking lot at the courthouse?"

"No, he did in the Remington Nature Reserve's parking lot before following you on the path."

Kate shuddered. "It was there all that time."

"Although he didn't exactly say it, I think he considered

setting it off several times. But he wanted his ex-wife's new address too much. Killing you wouldn't get him that."

"I'm so glad Janice and his kids are safe now."

"You're special, Kate. Every day I've fallen more and more in love with you."

She lowered her head and stared at her lap. "I never thought I would ever fall in love again, but I have. I should have told you something from the start, but everything was crazy around here."

He lifted her chin, so he could look into her eyes. "That's putting it mildly."

"I can't have any more children because of complications when Jamie was born. You'll make a great father, and I know you want kids, but I'm not the woman who can give them to you."

"Yes, I want a family, but I want you and Jamie more."

Tears glistened in Kate's eyes. "These are happy tears. Earlier today I didn't even know if I would see you or my son again. What I've gone through gives me even more of an understanding of what some battered women deal with on a daily basis. The loss of hope. The all-consuming fear from one moment to the next."

"This is the reason I love you. You're a protector, like me. I know you've been afraid for me during this case, but I'm doing what I was meant to do—like you. I was scared for you today, but we just have to put our lives in God's hands. I didn't think I could have it all. I wanted a wife and family. I saw how many of my buddies lit up when they talked about theirs. Thinking about them brought a ray of light into their lives even in the midst of war. Then when they died and I was left, a single man with no one back home waiting for me, I felt so guilty for surviving. But this past week, I've come to understand my purpose.

The Lord doesn't want us just to go through the motions of living, but to enjoy life, too."

Kate wiped the tears away and tugged his head toward hers. Her mouth settled over his, and Chase felt he had finally found a family to care for and love.

# EPILOGUE

*Nine months later*

Kate carried a birthday cake to the kitchen table where Jamie and Chase sat. "I know you're having a party tomorrow and will have another cake there, Jamie, but I wanted to celebrate your birthday with just the family tonight. You need to make a wish and blow these out."

With his wide eyes glued to the treat, Jamie stood up in his chair, leaned into the table and blew his two candles out. Grinning, he clapped his hands. "Me did it."

"Yes, you did, partner." Chase raised his hand for a high five, and Jamie slapped his palm against Chase's.

Jamie grabbed a fistful of cake and presented it to Chase. "For Dad-dy."

With her son at the end of the table, Kate sat across from her husband, cherishing the bond Jamie and Chase had. Although they hadn't even been married two months, her son already called Chase "Daddy."

He laughed and took a nibble. "Your mommy outdid herself with this cake." Chase's look captured Kate, and for a few seconds his love wrapped her in a cocoon of happiness.

Until her son tossed the rest of the cake still in his hand at her. His giggles resonated through the room. The chocolate that plonked onto the table after hitting her chest didn't bother her one bit. Jamie practiced his throwing anytime he could. He bent forward and stretched toward the platter again.

Kate quickly rose and picked the dessert up. "I'll cut the cake and take care of this." She gestured toward the bits of chocolate still clinging to her gray sweatshirt. "Will you clean him up?"

Chase picked Jamie up and carried him to the sink then gave Kate a wet washcloth for her sweatshirt.

Their son wiggled and pointed at Mac who had moseyed into the kitchen. "Down."

Chase set him on the floor, and Jamie toddled to Mac, plopped down next to him and laid his head against his side.

Kate put her arms around Chase's neck. "Good thing I married you when I did. Shuffling Mac between my house and yours was getting tiresome."

Chase laughed. "So that's why you agreed to marry me."

"Nope. This is why." Kate kissed her husband, pouring all her love into it.

\* \* \* \* \*

*If you liked this story, pick up these other stories from Margaret Daley:*

*THE YULETIDE RESCUE*
*TO SAVE HER CHILD*
*THE PROTECTOR'S MISSION*
*STANDOFF AT CHRISTMAS*
*HIGH-RISK REUNION*

*Available now from Love Inspired Suspense!*

*Find more great reads at www.LoveInspired.com.*

Dear Reader,

As a mother and grandmother, I could so easily put myself in Kate's shoes when she is protecting her son and searching for him. Something like that happening will really test your faith. But God is the only one who can really get you through a situation like that. He often sends people to help you. We were never meant to go through life alone.

I love hearing from readers. You can contact me at margaretdaley@gmail.com or at P. O. Box 2074, Tulsa, OK 74101. You can also learn more about my books at http://www.margaretdaley.com. I have a newsletter that you can sign up for on my website.

Take care,

Margaret Daley

For my wonderful editor, Elizabeth Mazer,
who continues to believe in my writing
and provided the opportunity to write this novella.

# YOUR PARTICIPATION IS REQUESTED!

Dear Reader,

Since you are a lover of our books – we would like to get to know you!

Inside you will find a short Reader's Survey. Sharing your answers with us will help our editorial staff understand who you are and what activities you enjoy.

To thank you for your participation, we would like to send you 2 books and 2 gifts – **ABSOLUTELY FREE!**

Enjoy your gifts with our appreciation,

*Pam Powers*

**SEE INSIDE FOR READER'S SURVEY**

For Your Reading Pleasure...

# YOUR READER'S SURVEY
## "THANK YOU" FREE GIFTS INCLUDE:
- ► 2 FREE books
- ► 2 lovely surprise gifts

## READER SERVICE—Here's how it works:

Accepting your 2 free Love Inspired® Suspense books and 2 free gifts (gifts valued at approximately $10.00) places you under no obligation to buy anything. You may keep the books and gifts and return the shipping statement marked "cancel." If you do not cancel, about a month later we'll send you 6 additional books and bill you just $5.24 each for the regular-print edition or $5.74 each for the larger-print edition in the U.S. or $5.74 each for the regular-print edition or $6.24 each for the larger-print edition in Canada. That is a savings of at least 13% off the cover price. It's quite a bargain! Shipping and handling is just 50¢ per book in the U.S. and 75¢ per book in Canada.* You may cancel at any time, but if you choose to continue, every month we'll send you 6 more books, which you may either purchase at the discount price plus shipping and handling or return to us and cancel your subscription. *Terms and prices subject to change without notice. Prices do not include applicable taxes. Sales tax applicable in N.Y. Canadian residents will be charged applicable taxes. Offer not valid in Quebec. Books received may not be as shown. All orders subject to approval. Credit or debit balances in a customer's account(s) may be offset by any other outstanding balance owed by or to the customer. Please allow 4 to 6 weeks for delivery. Offer available while quantities last.

If offer card is missing write to: Reader Service, P.O. Box 1867, Buffalo, NY 14240-1867 or visit www.ReaderService.com ▲

BUSINESS REPLY MAIL
FIRST-CLASS MAIL     PERMIT NO. 717     BUFFALO, NY

POSTAGE WILL BE PAID BY ADDRESSEE

READER SERVICE
PO BOX 1867
BUFFALO NY 14240-9952

NO POSTAGE
NECESSARY
IF MAILED
IN THE
UNITED STATES

# SAVED BY THE SEAL

Susan Sleeman

And my God will meet all your needs according to
the riches of His glory in Christ Jesus.
–*Philippians* 4:19

# ONE

$A$ hail of bullets peppered the outside of Bree Hatfield's house, piercing the wall.

She dove to the floor, her mind racing.

*Ella.* She had to get to the baby asleep in her portable crib.

*Father, please! Help me!*

Head down, Bree slithered across the room. The carpet's rough fibers burned her elbows, but she kept her gaze focused on Ella stirring in her crib.

Bullets continued to slice through the exterior wall. She cringed but kept moving. The window above her head exploded. Glass shards rained down, pricking her neck.

Her heart stuttered. She covered her head and tucked into a ball, freezing in place, hoping to escape a bullet.

*No! Ella needs me. She just lost her parents. I'm the only person she has now.*

Bree dug deeper for the resolve to move forward. She elbowed over the glass, the sharp shards piercing her skin. Pain radiated up her arms but she ignored it, powered ahead and reached the crib. She shot to her feet, lifted Ella and dropped back to the floor, all in one fluid motion.

She cradled Ella close. The baby's big blue eyes blinked hard. She puckered her mouth and let out a wailing cry as if she understood the looming danger.

"Shh, sweetie," Bree cooed as she turned on her side to protect the six-month-old. Bree stayed low and scooted forward, moving deeper into the house. She finally reached the cracked linoleum in the kitchen and slid behind the island of cabinets.

She let out a heavy sigh. Drew in a deeper breath and jiggled Ella to calm her while digging her cell phone from her pocket. With shaking fingers, she dialed.

"911. What's your emergency?" the operator asked.

"Help, please!" Bree cried out to be heard above Ella's cries. "Someone outside is shooting at my house."

"Your address?" the woman asked.

Bree rattled it off. "Hurry. Please. I have a baby here. She's in danger, too. I need help."

"Officers are on the way, ma'am. Are you in a secure location?"

"Secure? I don't know." Bree looked around the space. "I think so. As long as the shooter doesn't try to come inside."

The roar of a powerful engine sounded at the road followed by the squeal of tires.

"Wait. I think they're leaving." Bree listened. "The shooting. It's stopped."

"Stay where you are, ma'am, until the officers arrive."

"Yes…sure… I won't move."

"And hold on the line. I'll let you know when they arrive and it's safe to answer your door."

Ella's cries continued and tears rolled down her cheeks. Tears formed in Bree's eyes as well, and she wanted to wail with Ella. Instead, Bree kept rocking and wished she had Ella's pacifier. "Shh. Shh. It's okay, sweetie."

"How old is your daughter?" the operator asked, likely trying to calm Bree down.

The comment did just the opposite, as it reminded her

of Ella's parents who'd died two weeks ago from carbon monoxide poisoning. "She's six months old, but she's not my daughter. Her parents recently died, and I'll soon have full custody."

"I'm sorry for your loss."

"Thank you," Bree mumbled as she'd done over and over for the last two weeks when sympathies were offered on Laura's and Jason's deaths.

Such a terrible, horrible, senseless loss.

The day they died had started out so innocently. Ella was teething and cranky 24/7, so Bree had offered to watch the baby, allowing her friends to go out on their cabin cruiser and spend the night under the stars together, just the two of them.

But they didn't come home the next morning. Didn't answer their phones. Bree called 911, and the sheriff's department located their boat anchored in a secluded cove.

They were found in their bed, and the detective who investigated their deaths said the generator powering their air-conditioning failed, filling the cabin with carbon monoxide. An accidental death, he'd claimed, but Bree didn't believe it. Jason was too careful and meticulous with everything in life to die in such a preventable accident.

"Officers are just down the street," the operator said. "When they knock on your door it's safe to answer."

"Thank you." Bree sighed out a breath and disconnected.

She pushed to her knees to rock Ella who settled into more of a whimper than body-heaving cries. Still, Bree could use help with Ella as the police sorted out this disaster. Bree pressed the speed dial for her mother.

"Hey, sweetheart," her mother answered. "Ella fussy again?"

"Can you come over right away?" Bree fired off details

of the incident, her words shooting out as fast as the barrage of bullets that had cut through the wall.

"I'm on my way."

Not surprised at her mother's no-nonsense response, Bree disconnected. Her mother and she were both take-action kind of people. No point in dwelling on emotions and feelings or ruminating. Just face the problem head-on and solve it. That worked most of the time for Bree. Well, there was that one time with her former boyfriend Clint... but she wasn't going to let her mind go there.

She shoved her phone into her pocket and retrieved Ella's pacifier just before footsteps pounded toward her front stoop. Bree settled Ella in the crib and went to the door.

She found a young officer who looked barely old enough to shave. Behind him, another officer marched up to the neighboring house and a third officer rummaged in the trunk of his patrol car.

The officer at the door ran his gaze over her. "I'm Officer Winklemann. Is everyone all right here, ma'am?"

"We're fine." Bree rubbed her hand over her face.

"Your arms are bleeding."

She glanced at the cuts. "It's nothing. I'm a nurse. I can handle it."

The officer nodded and took out a small notebook. "Can you tell me your name and what happened here?"

She introduced herself. "I was getting ready for bed when all of a sudden someone started shooting."

"Did you see the shooter?"

She shook her head. "I dropped to the floor then crawled over to Ella's crib to move us behind the kitchen cabinets for safety. Then I called 911." How in the world was she organizing her thoughts when they were pinging around in her brain like pinballs?

"Do you know of anyone who would want to shoot at you or your house?"

Her thoughts immediately went to Laura's and Jason's deaths. Could this be related?

"Maybe. My friends died from carbon monoxide poisoning a few weeks ago." She shared the details. "I've been looking into the incident, and I'm beginning to think it wasn't an accident at all."

The officer's eyebrow went up in a perfect arc. "And why's that, ma'am?"

"First, there was a gouge on the boat, like another boat had rammed into it. Jason was meticulous about everything. If the gouge had happened before the day they died, he would have complained about the damage, and he didn't say a word. Second, I texted with Laura all day while they were on the boat. If it was damaged that day, she would have told me."

Officer Winklemann's eyes narrowed. "Okay, say the damage occurred near the time they died. It still doesn't mean someone killed them."

"There's more. After I discovered the gouge, I asked around the marina to see if anyone knew anything about another boat in the area that night. I found a guy who saw two boats in the cove tied together around the time they died. When he came closer to them, one boat raced off. He said it was too dark to describe the boat or the driver, but I asked the guy to the tell Detective Newlin about what he saw."

"And did he?"

She shook her head. "He refused. He said he was doing something that night that he didn't want the police to know about, and there was no way he'd go to them. I gave Detective Newlin the guy's name and boat registration number. Turns out the boat was stolen, and the detective couldn't find the guy. Detective Newlin thinks I'm just grasping at straws to get him to investigate when there's no real reason to do so."

"I can see why he might think that."

"I didn't make up my conversation with the guy, and he had no reason to lie to me about what he saw. Why would another boat be tied to Laura and Jason's in the middle of the night? And now this?" She gestured at her living room. "Look at this place. I think the killer followed me home and shot up the house. Maybe to warn me. Maybe to kill me."

The officer stared at her, his gaze patronizing. "You live on the fringe of a bad neighborhood, ma'am. This could simply be a drive-by shooting."

She glanced around the area, looking for anything to disprove her theory, but bullets had riddled only her home. "I see no damage to anything else from the shooting," she said. "It doesn't look like any other houses, or cars, or people out on the street were hit by the gunshots."

"Not that we can tell at this point," he admitted.

"But you expect me to believe that a random criminal drove by and decided to shoot up my house—and *only* my house—for absolutely no reason?" She sighed. "Why won't any of you listen to me?"

"From what you've told me, Detective Newlin did listen, and he investigated each incident you told me about, but he was unable to find anything that indicated foul play." The officer stared at her for a moment as if weighing his next move. "Still, I'll contact him and tell him about the shooting."

*Right, and tell him that you think I'm nuts while you're at it.*

"Make sure you also mention that I've been asking around at the dock, and I think the killer's afraid I'm on to him."

"Seems like a long shot, ma'am." He flipped his notebook closed. "We'll need you to remain in your house while we process the scene."

She nodded her understanding. "I called my mother. Marie Hatfield. She's on her way to help me with the baby. Can you please let her in?"

"Of course," he said and pivoted on his heel.

Bree watched him step down the walkway and talk with the officer at the patrol car. Together, they strung yellow tape across the road, sealing off her home as a crime scene. She wanted to think the officer was right, the detective, too, that Jason's and Laura's deaths were accidental, that no one was targeting her at all, but her gut said otherwise. It was clear, though, if someone killed Laura and Jason, it was up to her to prove it.

She stayed at the door watching her neighbors spill out of their houses and the officers take their statements. She stood strong under their cautious yet curious glances until her mother drove up. Bree wanted to collapse into her mother's arms as she'd done in her childhood, but she drew in a breath and blew it out instead. She was a mother now, and she had to be strong.

After showing her ID, her mother slipped under the fluttering yellow tape to march up the walk. Her expression tightened with each step.

She grabbed Bree up into a hug. "I'm so relieved you and Ella are okay."

"Me, too." Bree enjoyed the warm embrace for a moment then pushed away before she started getting weepy.

"It looks like a war zone out here," her mother said as they stepped inside and closed the door.

Bree ran a hand over her face.

Her mother took hold of Bree's arm. "You've cut yourself."

"I had to crawl through glass to get to Ella." Bree

checked the blood caked on her skin. She could treat herself, but the angle would prove a challenge. "Would you mind looking at it for me?"

"Sit and I'll get the first-aid kit."

Bree went to the sofa and shook the cushions. Glass tinkled to the floor, mixing with larger shards already underfoot. Thankfully, Bree hadn't crawled over any big pieces or her elbows would be shredded. She sat, her gaze going to the window, and her phone rang, startling her. She didn't recognize the caller's number, but she hoped it was someone she'd talked to at the marina and they had information on her friends' deaths.

She accepted the call. "Bree Hatfield."

"You're sticking your nose in where it doesn't belong," a gruff male voice said. "Back off or next time I'll make sure the bullets hit the mark."

Fear raced through Bree's veins, along with a sense of vindication. She'd been right after all. "Who is this?"

No response.

"Hello?" She looked at the screen to see the call had been disconnected.

Her mother came into the room. "You're as white as a sheet. What is it? What's happened?"

"I think I just got a call from Laura and Jason's killer."

"What?" Her mother dropped onto the table in front of Bree.

Bree ran her gaze over the broken vase, the shattered window, the wall filled with holes, and her fear ramped up. "He warned me to back off or next time he'd make sure he shot me."

Her mother twisted her hands together. "You need to tell the cops outside or get on the phone with that detective."

"And tell them what? That a man called and threatened me? The officer who took my statement thought I was way off mark, so he'll look at me like I'm crazy. And if the detective hasn't believed me so far, why will he believe this?"

"Good point, but you have to call him."

"I will," Bree replied, a sudden resolve filling her heart. "But even if he blows me off again, I have to keep looking for the killer. Ella's been left an orphan, and she deserves to know the truth about what happened to her parents. They deserve for the truth to be told, as well."

"Ella deserves to be safe, too," her mother pointed out. "How are you going to protect her and yourself from her parents' killer?"

"About that," Bree replied. "I have an idea."

Clint Reed rumbled down the country road in his 1950s Ford pickup that had once belonged to his granddad. The window open, he gulped in the late summer air. A born-and-bred Texan, there was something about the air in his home state that let him breathe deeper. Or maybe it had more to do with his lack of tension after leaving his crazy life as a navy SEAL behind for two weeks of leave on his ranch.

He turned off the highway and swung down the winding drive of HR Ranch, named after his granddad Hank Reed. Knee-high grasses, brown from the late summer sun, swished in the breeze. Clint called the ranch home for only a few weeks out of the year, but he'd been raised on the sprawling land since his parents died when he was twelve.

The tires crunched over gravel, taking him past a large corral that brought childhood memories flooding back. Riding his horse in this very corral. Climbing the big oak at the end of the drive and building a tree house. His stern grandfather who failed to show love, always judging. Making life hard on a boy whose parents had been the very opposite. Making Clint hate the place.

Still, now that his granddad had passed and the HR belonged to Clint, he found peace on the acreage—especially when he needed a break from the extreme demands of his job. The solitude away from people, from life-threatening problems and missions. Give him a few days at the HR riding his horses, Frosty and Trident, and he'd gladly head back to the SEALs for his next deployment.

He rounded a bend and spotted lights shining through the trees.

Lights? Was someone at the house?

He stomped on the brakes to think before going barreling up to the house. His housekeeper, Nessie, could be there, he supposed, but not likely at ten o'clock at night. He killed his headlights and cut off the engine before dialing her.

"Allgood residence," she answered.

"It's Clint. Are you at the ranch?"

"No."

"When's the last time you were here?"

"Yesterday."

"Did you leave a light on for me?

"No."

"Anything seem odd when you were here?"

"No."

Most of the time Clint appreciated Nessie's to-the-point personality, but right now, he'd like more than one-word answers. "And Pete? Is he here?"

"He's snoring up a storm in his recliner, but we'll be over first thing in the morning."

"Okay. See you then." Clint disconnected.

Had Nessie actually left a light on? She was conscientious, and yet, she was nearing seventy. He needed to check it out, and he'd been a SEAL far too long not to take care and approach under cover.

He silenced his phone and slipped out of the truck, glad the door's rusty hinges were quiet for once. He unlocked the tool box in the truck bed to retrieve his handgun and rifle.

He loaded both guns and set off for the house, moving silently through the trees. A soft breeze played over the tranquil ranch, cutting through the sticky night alive with cricket chirps and an owl's repeated hoots. Everything in nature was ignorant of the danger that lurked ahead, but Clint wouldn't let down his guard.

In the clearing around the long, low house, he found an older-model sedan. He eased alongside it for cover and took a good look.

*What in the world?*

He moved closer and ran his fingers over bullet holes dotting the side. His apprehension skyrocketed.

Was a local thug using the usually empty house as a hideout? Clint would have installed a security system, but he'd never had any issues. Plus Nessie and Pete didn't like the thought of having to arm and disarm it, so he'd bowed to their wishes. Maybe it was time to reconsider.

He racked his handgun and continued forward, working his way through tall grasses and wildflowers to the mowed area outside the house. Warm light spilled out, illuminating the shrubs and flowers Nessie cared for. Gauzy curtains fluttered in the breeze and brought him to a stop.

So the window was open. Nessie might have left a light on but she would never leave a window open. Something moved behind the curtains. Someone was inside and he needed to find out who.

His best bet was to enter through the back door and surprise them. He circled around the rear of the house, unlocking the door as quietly as he could. He slipped in-

side and down the hall where female voices drifted out
to meet him.

One voice pierced his brain, and his heart skipped a
beat.

*No.* He had to be wrong. *She* couldn't be here. Right?

He shot a quick look into the room and spotted two
women. He recognized both of them but the younger
woman's face was burned into his memory.

So now what? How did he step into the room and tell
the only woman he'd ever loved that he was home without
letting her see how much she still got to him?

*Keep it light.* That's what he'd do. He cleared his throat
to alert them to his presence.

"Hi, honey, I'm home," he joked as he swung around
the corner.

"What on earth." Bree clutched her chest. "What are
*you* doing here?"

"Ah, this is my house, Bree. Shouldn't I be the one asking that question and demanding a good reason for you
breaking in?"

She rushed across the room to him, tears filling her
eyes. "I'm in trouble, Clint. Big trouble, and I have nowhere else to go."

Aw, man. No. Not tears. Not a voice that trembled with
fear. He could tune out a lot of things in life, but he could
never ignore a woman in trouble, especially not when the
woman was Bree.

# TWO

Bree managed to hide her shock at seeing Clint, but just barely.

"Marie," he greeted Bree's mother with a smile, and Bree couldn't take her eyes off him.

He hadn't changed much. Over six feet tall, his shoulders were broad in the plaid shirt open over a white T-shirt, his jeans as worn as his favorite old pair of boots. He had a thick head of shaggy brown hair with copper highlights, but it was his eyes that drew her attention just as they had the six months they'd been together. Brown in color, they changed according to his moods. Dark coffee brown when he was irritated or concerned as he was now, but a warm chocolate when she caught him gazing at her with the affection they'd once shared.

Oh, man. He was here. Really and truly here, and she'd all but run into his arms for help when he'd stepped into the room.

Why hadn't she prepared herself to handle the possibility of seeing him again? She'd been consumed with the need to protect Ella and find a killer, she supposed. Or maybe she didn't want to think about Clint. They hadn't been together since she'd called things off three years earlier. Not that she didn't want to be with him, but she couldn't. As a nurse in the war zone in Iraq, she'd seen the horrors that he faced on a regular basis. She could never be with a man, start a family with a man who put himself in such danger. She should trust God to keep Clint safe, but every time he had deployed when they'd been together, fear had consumed her.

Still, in all that time, she hadn't been able to forget him. She measured every man she met against him, and they all fell short in comparison.

Ella's sharp cry sounded from the bedroom, and Clint spun in that direction, his gun coming up in his hand. Ever the SEAL. Cementing in her mind why they couldn't be together.

"Relax. It's just Ella," Bree's mother said. "I'll go get her."

She didn't wait for Bree to agree, but stepped into the hallway.

"You have a baby?" Anguish rode though Clint's voice.

"You think I…no, wait…she's mine, but not mine. My friends. Jason and Laura. You remember them?"

He nodded.

"They died, leaving me custody of Ella. That's why I'm here. To protect Ella."

As if Ella knew Bree was talking about her, her crying wound down until Bree could no longer hear her.

Clint stepped closer, his eyes warming. "I'm sorry for your loss. I know how much you loved them."

The tenderness and compassion in his tone wrapped around her as tears pricked her eyes. She wasn't normally a crier, but after everything that had happened the last few weeks, tears threatened all the time.

She firmed her shoulders to ward them off. "I did love them, which is why I have to find the person who killed them."

"Killed them? They were murdered?"

She nodded. "And the police won't believe me."

He watched her for a moment, before gesturing at the sofa. "Let's sit and you can tell me what's going on."

She moved to the far end of the plaid sofa and hoped he got the hint to put some space between them and sit on the other end. Of course, he didn't. He dropped onto the heavy oak coffee table right in front of her and leaned his elbows on his knees, his gaze raptly fixed to her face.

How could she think with him looking at her like that?

*Get a grip. If not for your sake, then for Ella's. Just stick to the facts.*

"Ella is teething and has been pretty cranky, totally stressing out her parents," she said. "I offered to watch her for a day so they could spend the night on their boat. There's evidence that the generator they'd used to power the AC malfunctioned. They died of carbon monoxide poisoning. Their deaths were ruled an accident."

"But you don't agree."

She shook her head then shared everything that had happened. "To be fair to the detective, it's all just my word. And I acted out when he first told me they died, so I can see why he might not trust me. But I have to figure out what really happened."

"That's not a good idea," Clint said. "You could become a victim, too."

"That's why we're here. After the call from the killer I know he's serious about hurting me. Your ranch is the safest place for Ella, my mom and me."

"Then my house is yours for as long as you need it." He sat up straight and a firm look of resolve crossed his face. "And now that I know you're in danger, I'm not going to let anything bad happen to any of you. You have my word on it."

"Are you sure you want us to stay?" She met his gaze head on. "With the stress of your job I know you need peace and quiet when you're on leave and having a baby around won't give you that."

He pulled back his shoulders, taxing the seam of his shirt. "We may not have been able to make a go of things between us, but I still care about you, and I'm not going to leave your side until I'm sure you're safe."

Even if she wanted to argue with him—which she didn't—once his mind was made up about something there was no swaying him.

"Thank you." She smiled.

He returned her smile but shifted to watch her mother enter the room carrying Ella. "If you'll take her, I'll go find the teething gel."

Bree took the precious child and cuddled her close, smelling her baby-soft hair as she whimpered. Bree reminded herself that every day going forward, everything was for Ella. For making her life better. Easier. And raising her as her parents had wanted.

Ella stiffened and started to wail.

Clint frowned and looked at her like she was an alien. "You don't expect help with the baby, right?"

"Right," she replied, but sadness creased her heart.

Nothing had changed. Clint still didn't want children. She did. One of the reasons they'd split up. Now she had a daughter, and he looked like an invading army was marching through the room, and he wanted to flee.

Bree forced her attraction and feelings for Clint aside and drew Ella closer to soothe her. Ella had to come first, and Bree couldn't be interested in any relationship until she stabilized her life. That wouldn't happen until the killer was caught. And even once that happened, she couldn't be interested in a man like Clint who not only didn't want children, but wouldn't be around to help raise them.

Bree walked the floor with the fussy baby and Clint tracked Bree's every move. Tall and thin, she had the look of a runner, which she was. She often wore athletic attire on her days off and was kind of a tomboy with her brown hair usually worn in a ponytail, accenting expressive brown eyes. Clint had always gone for more feminine women, but something about Bree had hooked him the moment they met.

Maybe it was the way she looked at him, at others, like she knew what they were going through and hoped to ease their distress.

Ella suddenly tossed back her head and screamed at the top of her lungs. Apparently the teething gel hadn't kicked in yet or wasn't working at all. Clint wanted to help, but Bree was far more capable than he was of settling the child. He could already tell she was a great mom, just as he'd always known she would be.

He wanted a wife and children. Several kids, in fact. But he wouldn't get married until it was time for him to transition into a job that allowed him to be present in his child's life instead of being deployed. He knew the pain of being raised without parents. He would never inflict that same pain on his own child.

Sure, he could leave the SEALs, but he was called to help others. While he had the health and stamina to continue his work, he had an obligation to see it through. To serve where he felt he could do the most good. Even if it meant he couldn't be with Bree.

When she'd come into his life, he'd prayed for God's direction, and no other job that he was suited for had presented itself. So as long as he worked as a SEAL, he had to accept the restrictions the job placed on his life. No wife or family for him.

Bree swayed with Ella until she quieted down. "Hopefully the teething gel is working, and we will all be able to get some sleep. Sorry, but I chose the biggest room so I could keep Ella nearby. I suspect it's your bedroom. We can move."

He waved a hand. "I'll just need to grab a few things, and I can sleep anywhere."

"I suppose as a SEAL you have to be able to do that."

He nodded.

"Are things still going well in the job?"

He took a moment before responding as he wasn't sure exactly what she wanted to know. "If you're asking if I'm ready to leave it, nothing has changed. I believe this is God's will for my life right now."

A flash of pain lit in her eyes then vanished as fast as it appeared. He liked seeing that it still bothered her that they couldn't be together. Not a good thing to admit, but it might mean she, like he, hadn't let go of what they'd had together.

Not something he should be thinking about. He needed to move to a safer topic. "Since you're gung ho about finding this killer, do you have any thoughts on where to start looking?"

"Let me put Ella down, and then we can talk about it." She started around the couch.

"Do you need any help?"

She shot him a look over her shoulder. "You want to help?"

"I may not be ready to have children, but I didn't say

I disliked them." Especially when they were absolutely adorable and had big eyes and plump cheeks like Ella's.

"Right," she replied.

Sadness deepened her tone. Man, it hurt to hear her pain, and he wanted to reach out to her. Another bad idea. Maybe he should rethink staying here with her. His friend Shawn Dunlop was a local deputy, and he'd probably agree to watch out for her and look into the murder.

*No.* Not happening. He wasn't leaving her safety to Shawn or anyone else. He was the most skilled person here, and taking charge right now might make up for some of the pain he'd caused her when they'd broken things off. He'd just have to suck it up and not let his feelings get to him. He knew how to do that. He'd done it with his grandfather for years, each and every time he'd voiced his anger over being forced to leave the job he loved to care for a kid.

Clint could employ these coping skills he'd learned with his granddad to get through this time with Bree.

She breezed back into the room, a soft smile on her face, and dropped onto the sofa. "Each time I conquer one of Ella's teething episodes and get her down to sleep again, I feel like I'm taken one step closer to being a real mom."

"I have no doubt you're a wonderful mother."

She sighed. "I still have so much to figure out. I took a short leave from work, but I have to go back eventually." She frowned. "I wish I could stay home with her like Laura did, but I have to support us somehow."

"But first you'll investigate her death. How do you plan to go about it?"

"I'll leave Ella here with Mom. No one knows where we are so she'll be safe. Then I'll head back to the marina to see if I can find Adam Carpenter again. He's the guy who said he saw two boats that night."

"Sounds like finding him might be a long shot, but we have to try."

"We, as in you're coming with me?"

He couldn't tell if she liked or loathed the idea. "I told you I'd keep you safe. That means not letting you out of my sight."

"I appreciate that."

"And I want to get a look at your friends' boat, too. After my years in the navy, maybe I can see something you and the police missed."

A hopeful gleam filled her eyes. "Do you really think you'll find something?"

"If the detective—what's his name again?"

"Greg Newlin."

"Right, so if Newlin doesn't really believe your friends were murdered, he might not be looking at the boat as he would a crime scene."

"Good point."

"Not that I'm skilled in processing a crime scene, but I've been trained to carefully evaluate my surroundings. I also have a buddy who's a local deputy. If we strike out tomorrow, maybe I can get him to take a look at the boat, too."

"That would be wonderful."

He sat back to think about the situation. "We need to try to figure out why someone would want to kill Laura and Jason. Why don't you tell me more about them? Their jobs, things like that."

"Jason was an insurance adjuster for some big health insurance company. Laura used to be a nurse, too. We met at work, but she quit a little over a year ago to nurse her mother who had terminal cancer. She died a few months before Ella was born. Laura never went back to work, but stayed home with Ella."

"Okay, so this isn't about Laura's job, but could be about Jason's. Or maybe it has to do with Laura's mother. Do you know if Laura might have inherited anything valuable?"

"No. Laura and I talked about her mother, and all her money was used for her medical bills. In fact, Laura was helping pay for them at the end."

"And Jason's job?"

"He didn't talk about it. Not ever."

"Didn't you find that odd?"

She shrugged. "It didn't seem odd at the time. Insurance isn't really fun to talk about."

"Did he or Laura ever say he disliked his job?"

Bree shook her head.

"Did you ever meet any of his coworkers?"

"No, he didn't hang out with them outside of work. He was an introvert and a real homebody except for when he was boating. He really didn't have any friends other than Laura's friends."

"Still, we should consider talking to his coworkers. Family members, too."

"Laura and Jason didn't have any living family. That's why they gave me custody of Ella. I'm executor of the estate so I have access to the house. Maybe we can find information about his work there."

"Okay, so we'll start at the marina tomorrow, and if time allows, we'll stop by their house."

She frowned and twisted her hands in her lap. "I was staying there with Ella the night they died. I gathered up her things and haven't gone back."

"Are you up to it?" He reached out to take her hands and offer comfort.

She moved back. "I'll do whatever it takes to find their killer."

And that was what was twisting Clint's gut into a knot. Bree cared deeply about people and she always sacrificed herself for them. Seemed like she planned to do whatever she could to find her friend's killer, even if it meant sacrificing her life.

# THREE

The next morning in the kitchen, Clint watched Bree feed Ella. Bree wore a plain sundress with a blue jean jacket and cowboy boots. As if he didn't like her enough already, he had a soft spot for women who wore boots as his mother had often done.

Ella had big globs of a goopy-looking cereal down the front of her bib and on a little one-piece number with pink kites and blue balloons. She raised a fist and shoved it in her mouth, then pulled it out with mushy drool covering her fingers.

"She eats like most of the guys on my SEAL team." Clint laughed.

He waited for Bree to laugh with him, but she frowned.

"What'd I say?" he asked.

"Nothing. It's just, when Laura fed Ella, she didn't make a mess like this."

"The kid and her clothes are washable, right? So it's no big deal."

"Exactly," Marie stepped into the room and peered up at him. "I keep telling Bree to stop comparing herself to Laura as there's no point in it."

Bree tapped her forehead. "I get that up here, but my heart's not quite on board yet."

"You want what's best for Ella, and that will win out no matter if she gets messy or not." Marie bent over Ella. "Right, sweetie? You're a big old mess, and we don't care."

Ella gave Marie a huge toothless grin and drool mixed with food oozed out and slid down to her bib.

"Go ahead and make things worse." Bree stood and handed the food bowl to Marie. "You're the one who will be cleaning her up afterward."

"Seems like that smile was worth it, though," Clint said.

"Et tu, Brute?" Bree asked then laughed. "Let me wash this cereal off my hands and grab my purse, then I'm ready to go."

He watched her leave, her skirt swishing with each step.

Marie sat in the chair vacated by Bree. "Bree still seems fond of you. If the way you're looking at her says anything, you feel the same way."

He wasn't aware his feelings were so transparent. He'd best get a better handle on them.

"A piece of advice?" she asked.

"Sure, why not."

"Life is short. Jason's and Laura's deaths only proves that. If you and my daughter care for each other, then maybe you should work through whatever came between you."

"It's not that simple."

"Isn't it?"

"Isn't what?" Bree asked as she returned carrying a large purse.

"Nothing." Clint gestured toward the door.

She eyed him for a moment then changed her focus to her mother. "I'll have my cell so make sure to call with any problems."

"I do know how to take care of a baby. You were once one, you know."

Clint laughed, and Bree scowled at him.

Okay, fine. Taking her mom's side two times in less than ten minutes probably wasn't a good idea before heading out to spend the whole day with her. Or maybe it was. That scowl would help him ignore how glad he was to see her again.

Not that it seemed to matter what he did, as she remained silent for the thirty-minute trip to the marina. Only when they approached the turnoff did she seem to remember he was in the truck with her.

She pointed at a sign announcing their arrival at the county park. "Just follow the signs, and you can't miss it."

Clint turned onto the marina road. "Has Jason always owned a boat?"

"He inherited it from his dad about five years ago." Her eyes narrowed. "I've been thinking that if you had asked me before they died about how well I knew Jason, I would have said we were very close friends. But now I'm realizing how much I didn't know about him."

"Is the same thing true of Laura?"

Bree shook her head, and the braid running down her back swung in response. "I'll be surprised if there's anything I learn about her that I don't already know."

"Her death must be hard on you."

"I keep reaching for my phone to text or call her and then remember I can't." She swiveled to face him. "But you'd know all about that after losing your mom and dad."

He nodded, but didn't elaborate as he didn't want to add to the already somber mood. He pointed at the sign ahead. "We're here."

She changed her focus out the window, and he pulled into the parking lot. Even on a Monday morning, fishing boats, wave runners and cabin cruisers all mixed together in bright colors bobbing on the cool blue water.

"It's funny." He shifted into Park and stared over the lake. "I was never much for the water until I joined the navy."

"Then why did you enlist?"

"At the time, I wanted to be anywhere but on the miles and miles of land in Texas, and I thought adventures on the high seas sounded exciting."

"From what you were cleared to tell me about your job, you've lived a very adventurous life."

He grinned at her. "You don't know the half of it."

Her forehead furrowed. "So just to be clear, are you staying with the SEALs because it's a calling or because you think you'd die of boredom here in Texas?"

"It's a calling," he replied quickly, but didn't explain that if it was just for the thrills, he'd have gladly given up the excitement for her. "We should get going. Wait here until I check things out, okay?"

"Sure."

He climbed out and made a quick sweep of the parking lot. He patted the holster under his jacket and was glad he had a concealed carry permit allowing him to carry a handgun. He opened her door and stood back. She slid long slender legs from the truck.

He dragged his focus back to the surroundings. "Stay close to me."

"Sure."

They crossed the lot to a wooden walkway leading out to a low-slung metal building holding the marina office and a small restaurant.

"Do we have to check in with the office before seeing the boat?" he asked.

"No. I have the keys. Follow me and I'll show you where it is."

She continued down the walkway to the covered boat

storage area. It made perfect sense to Clint that the meticulous Jason wouldn't leave his boat exposed to the elements in an uncovered slip. She turned off on one of the docks and stopped beside a white boat with a blue-and-red stripe running around the hull. Clint didn't know much about cabin cruisers, but he recognized the high-end brand.

"Expensive boat," he said.

"Laura told me Jason's father had expensive tastes." She stood staring down at the platform on the boat's stern where they would board.

"I should have thought to wear athletic shoes." She shrugged. "I'll just have to take these off."

"Boots can be tricky to pull off while standing. Let me help."

Before she could object, he knelt at her feet and took one foot in his hands.

To keep from falling, she had no choice but to rest a hand on his shoulder. He should have thought this through, as her touch felt like a hot branding iron.

He removed both boots and forced out a smile. "Now my turn."

She started to bend down.

"Don't worry, I can handle my own boots." He sat to remove them.

She didn't argue but stepped onto the boat.

Clint joined her. "What is this? A thirty footer?"

She shrugged. "I think that's what Jason said, but I didn't really pay much attention to the little details he shared and I personally know nothing about boats."

"I've had a little bit of experience with them." He winked to try to keep things light between them.

"Of course you have." She turned away, and he wondered if he'd said something wrong. "What do you want to see first?"

"The cabin."

She opened the gate to the outdoor seating area, and then unlocked the cabin door. Clint was thankful he could stand upright in the cabin and still have a few inches to spare. Bree stopped moving to stare at the bow of the boat where a dining table and benches were folded down into a bed, likely the spot where the couple had died.

She took a breath and blew it out, but her shoulders started shaking. He soon heard her sniffle.

He should stay far away from her, but he couldn't let her cry without offering comfort. He rested a hand on her shoulder. "It's got to be hard to come down here."

She pivoted to look up at him. Anguish lingered in tear-filled eyes, and she looked as helpless as little Ella had appeared the night before.

"Aw, honey, don't." He didn't think but drew her into his arms. "I'm so sorry."

She rested her head against his chest, and her crying intensified. Her touch on his shoulder earlier had sent him reeling, but holding her again made his head spin. But this wasn't about him. It was about her and comforting her in her grief.

"Shh," he whispered and stroked her back until her sobs lessened, and she simply lay with her head against his chest.

She suddenly pushed back. "I'm sorry. I don't know what came over me."

He resisted reaching out to swipe lingering tears from her high cheeks. "It takes time to heal from such a loss."

"I suppose." She cleared the remaining tears with her own fingers. "But you're not here to help me through that so we should get started on what we came to do."

She spun. Good. He didn't want her to see that he was very ready to help her through her grief. Not the right thing to do when he couldn't be there for her any more today than three years ago. He wished things were different, but wishing never changed anything. If it did, with all his childhood wishing, his parents would still be alive.

He stepped through the plush cabin with a small kitchen, bathroom and another small berth, running his gaze over every inch as he moved. Coming up with nothing to help, he faced Bree. "I'm assuming the generator's in the engine hatch on the deck. Do you know how to open the hatch?"

"I saw Detective Newlin do it. There's a switch on a console outside. I'll show you."

On deck, she went straight to the helm station holding switches and gauges. She put the key in the ignition and pressed the hatch switch. He waited for the floor to rise up, but it didn't move.

She looked up. "It's not budging, and I know it works."

He stepped over to the station and checked the gauges. "The battery's almost dead."

Looking frustrated, she dropped into the helm seat. "So now what?"

"We have two options that I can think of. We could use a car battery to power the hatch—which I don't feel good about doing because I don't know the electrical system on this boat. Option two is that most boats have a way to open the hatch manually. There should be access to the release pin under the table base or in the seating storage."

"Let's try that."

"Full disclosure, I could damage something and you might want to get a mechanic out here instead of me messing with it."

"We can't wait for that."

"I'll need tools."

She retrieved Jason's toolkit. "Can I help at all?"

"In a minute, I'll need your assistance in lifting the

hatch." He set to work releasing the pin. The hatch popped up a fraction of an inch.

"Okay, now's when I need your help." He got into position to lift the door, and she stepped to the other end. "It's going to be heavy so get a good grip and be prepared for the weight."

She nodded and slipped her fingers under the end.

"Ready?" He braced his knees to take the brunt of the weight. "Lift."

When they raised the door about a foot, movement caught his eye.

"What the…" He suddenly recognized the thing that was moving. "Drop the door and jump back!"

"What?"

"Now, Bree! Drop it."

She gave him a puzzled look but let go and stepped back as he released his hold.

The door slammed to the deck. Clint quickly moved to seal the gasket, closing off the hatch completely.

"What's wrong?" she asked.

"A Texas coral snake was slithering toward your hand."

"A snake?"

"Not just any snake. It's the most poisonous snake in the US. It carries neurotoxins and could easily kill you."

Her eyes went wide, and she shot a look around. "A snake…poisonous…but how? Who?"

This wasn't a snake typically found around water, but Clint had a pretty good idea of how it had gotten into the sealed waterproof hatch.

The killer.

Bree watched the animal control worker carry the container off the boat. He'd removed a total of three snakes, and she could hardly breathe for how close she'd come to being bitten.

She sighed, catching Clint's attention. His warm gaze was like a caress, reminding her of being held by him a few hours ago. Having his arms around her again had felt like she'd found something important that she'd been missing, and part of her wished he'd repeat his performance right now.

But why? What good would it do? She still wanted him by her side, not off in some foreign country. Sure, when they'd dated they'd been able to regularly communicate via video and telephone, but she couldn't hug a phone or computer—not if she wanted to receive any warmth or affection in return.

Clint looked at his watch. "It's almost lunchtime. Why don't you show me the gouge, and then we'll regroup over lunch at the marina restaurant."

She stepped to the far side of the boat where she pointed at the long blue gash in the otherwise pristine white paint.

Clint leaned over the edge next to her. "Looks like there's enough paint left behind to take a sample and get it analyzed."

"To what end?"

"My deputy friend Shawn once told me that samples from cars can be matched to paint colors used by automobile manufacturers. That then gives the police a model to look for. Maybe they can do the same thing with boats."

"That would be wonderful."

Clint sat up. "When you were questioning people, did you ask if anyone could identify the type of boat that would leave such a mark?"

"I don't understand."

"Since boats are various sizes and designs they ride

differently in the water. It would take a certain size boat to cause damage this high up."

"I had no idea, but we could stop at the office and talk to Dennis Green. He's the marina manager and seems to know a lot about boats."

"Sounds like a plan."

On the dock, they slipped into their boots and, as they started down walkway, she spotted Dennis's snowy white hair as he worked on one of the moorings.

"Excuse me, Mr. Green," she called out and rushed down the dock toward him.

Clint hurried up next to her, and she appreciated his protective instincts.

Dennis wiped his hands on his shorts and peered up at her. "Ms. Hatfield. Seems like there was quite a commotion on your boat this morning."

"Yes." She avoided giving him details by quickly introducing Clint, but didn't offer his profession. She'd seen firsthand how knowing Clint was a SEAL intimidated people, and she wanted Dennis to speak freely. "I was wondering if any of your boaters have snakes as pets."

"Snakes? My word." He sat back on his haunches and straightened the collar on his knit shirt. "Is that why animal control was at your boat?"

She nodded.

"I don't know of anyone into snakes, and I've never seen anyone bring them onboard."

"If you do hear something, would you let me know?"

"Of course." He turned back to the post he'd been working on.

"One more thing," she said, garnering his attention again. "If you looked at the gouge I told you about on Jason's boat, might you be able to give us an idea of what type of boat could have done the damage?"

He pushed up his rimless glasses. "Sure. I could at least make an educated guess on the size of the boat, but you should know there are a ton of models so narrowing it down might be difficult."

"Still, any help you could give would be appreciated." She led him straight to the gouge, not even stopping to take off her boots. Clint stayed on the dock, his gaze roving over the area.

Dennis gave her feet a disdainful look, but joined her at the gouge. He studied it for a few moments then pulled back. "Let me look at it from the slip next door."

He disembarked and they followed him to the dock running parallel with the other side of Jason's boat.

"Okay, I can tell you the damage came from a much larger boat. I'd say you're looking at a forty footer, or even bigger." He rattled off a few boat models, and Bree jotted them down on a notepad from her purse.

"Could you suggest any specific models moored here?" Clint asked.

"Sure, but I don't want to at all intimate that one of the boats at the marina caused the damage. We have a public boat ramp, too, so anyone could have been on the water when this happened."

"Could you give us a list of the boats moored here?"

He shook his head hard. "Privacy rules and all."

"But you wouldn't mind if we looked around at the boats, right?" Clint drew back his shoulders, and Bree knew it would take a strong man to say no to Clint at any time, but when he looked like a fierce warrior as he was doing now it would be nigh on impossible.

Dennis chewed on the inside of his cheek for a moment then met Bree's gaze head on. "Stick to the docks and no trespassing on the boats. I've had some complaints from our customers about you asking so many questions so I'd prefer if you didn't bother anyone else."

"I'll do my very best not to," Bree said truthfully, but she knew she would follow up on any promising lead they turned up.

"How many slips do you have here?" Clint asked.

"Five hundred, and most of them are filled."

Clint let out a low whistle then peered at Bree. "We should get started then."

Bree bid Dennis goodbye, and then she and Clint stepped off.

"Do you really think we'll find the killer's boat here?" she asked.

"I think if we do, odds are good that the damage from the paint rubbing off has been repaired by now so we won't easily be able to prove it hit Jason's boat. At least if I was the killer, I'd have fixed it before anyone started asking questions."

"So is it even worth our time to look?"

He nodded. "Once we locate potential boats, we can follow up on registration numbers and that will help us track down the owners and maybe even repairs."

"But we don't have access to that kind of information."

"I have my sources," he said, and she knew without a doubt, if the information was available, Clint would find a way to get it.

# FOUR

Late in the afternoon, when Bree and Clint took a refreshment break, Bree sipped her iced tea on the deck outside the marina restaurant. The restaurant floated on the water and soft waves bumped the platform in soothing, rhythmic movements, but Bree couldn't relax. Not after finding a trio of poisonous snakes on the boat that morning.

They'd notified Detective Newlin, and by the time they'd finished speaking with Dennis, Newlin had sent out a forensic team who processed the deck and hatch for leads. Newlin had also made a quick appearance but left without saying anything to aid their search. Their only recourse had been the footwork Clint had suggested, walking around the slips and identifying large boats painted blue. They'd located three of them that met their criteria of size and color, but only one of them held any damage that could have been from ramming Jason's boat. After a brief break, they were going to ask marina staff for the owners' names. Bree was all for the questioning, but she felt uneasy at being out in the open when a killer might be after her.

She peered at Clint. "You don't think the killer will try to hurt me in broad daylight with so many witnesses around, do you?"

"I don't think anyone will attack you head-on, but after

the snakes, I won't let my guard down." Clint met her gaze and held it. "You're too important to me to let anything happen to you."

She didn't know how to respond to the open admission of his feelings when he rarely expressed them, so she didn't. "We should move on to our questioning so I can get back to the ranch and take over Ella's care."

He stood. "You seem to be handling your sudden parenthood pretty well."

"Only because Mom is helping me."

"It looks to me like you're a natural and should have that house full of kids you always dreamed of." He gestured for her to go ahead of him.

"Even if I could handle more than one child—which at the moment I can't—I wouldn't choose to have more children without being married."

"Any prospects?" he asked so quietly she looked at him to be sure he'd spoken. "A guy, I mean."

She shook her head. "How about you? Is there a woman in your life?"

He shook his head but didn't expound. She irrationally hoped that meant he hadn't gotten over her as she hadn't gotten over him, but she wasn't going to ask.

She pointed at a worker ahead. "There's someone we can talk to."

She dug out her phone so she could display the photos she'd taken of the boats they'd located.

"Excuse me." She held out her phone. "Could you tell me who owns these boats?"

The guy let her display each picture for him, but then looked up, his eyes narrowed. "Sorry. The manager would fire me if I gave out any information, and I need my job."

As much as Bree wanted to push, she didn't want the

man to lose his job so she thanked him and moved down the dock until they reached another worker who was washing a boat.

She followed the same procedure and got the same response.

As they moved on, she sighed.

"Hey," Clint said. "There's going to be someone here who knows something and is willing to share. It's just a matter of odds."

Their next worker was a young woman, and Bree quickly explained their mission.

The woman eyed Bree. "You're that lady who's been asking around about Jason, right?"

Bree nodded.

"I'm sorry about your friends. They were good people." She frowned. "I can't tell you anything about the boats or I could lose my job, but I did see Jason arguing with one of owners the week he died."

"Can you tell us who it was?"

She shook her head. "I probably shouldn't have even said as much as I did."

"So why did you?" Clint asked.

She peered up at Clint. "'Cause I liked Laura and Jason."

"If you liked them so much, why not give us some names?"

She cupped her hand over her eyes and nodded down the docks. "Sorry, but Mr. Green is staring at us, and I have to get back to work." She turned away.

"Looks like I was wrong," Clint said to Bree. "We're not going to get any information with Green watching like a hawk. We're better off heading back to the ranch where I can research these registration numbers."

Bree felt like they were giving up, but she needed to

give her mother a break, and they could always return to the marina tomorrow.

Back at the ranch, Clint parked in front of the house. An older man wearing threadbare jeans, dusty boots and a stained white cowboy hat stormed across the yard.

"That's Pete," Clint said. "He's the ranch hand I mentioned this morning."

"He looks mad."

"That's just Pete. He's a grumbling old guy, but he has a good heart if you can stick around long enough to see it." Clint chuckled. "C'mon, I'll introduce you."

"With his look, I'm not sure I want to meet him."

"You'll charm him like you do everyone."

She stepped down from the truck and waited with Clint for Pete to arrive.

"Someone cut a fence on the east side of the property." The words flew from Pete's mouth as soon as he was in speaking range. He eyed her as if he thought she was guilty of the crime.

"I certainly didn't do it," she said.

"Pete, this is my friend, Bree," Clint said. "She's not the kind of person who goes around cutting holes in fences."

Pete ran his gaze from her boots to her head and back down again. "City slicker pretending to be a rancher."

Bree forced a smile to her lips. "I am at that."

His mouth dropped open.

"I'm pretty good on a horse if that helps you to accept that I'm staying here."

"Some." As if he'd dismissed her already, he changed his focus to Clint. "I mended the fence and didn't see any other damage."

He spun and marched off as fast as he arrived.

"I'm going to call him Tornado Pete," Bree said.

"A fitting name." But Clint's smile at her comment soon morphed into a frown.

"What's wrong?"

"I don't like that the fence was cut when you're running from a killer."

"It's likely just a coincidence, right?"

He eyed her. "I don't believe in coincidences, Bree, and I caution you not to as well."

Dinner over, Clint strolled beside Bree as she carried Ella on a short walk. The baby's gaze roved over the area, her big eyes opening wider. Clint once had the same kind of enthusiasm for the ranch. Before his parents died. Then without his parents' love, the place had felt like a prison.

A thought he wasn't going to waste a beautiful evening on. He gazed over his property and tried to see it from Ella or Bree's eyes. Ahead sat the combo barn and stable, the new metal roof glowing in the fading sun, the worn wood walls attesting to the age of the structure. Next to it sat a large paddock where his childhood horse, Frosty, grazed. Trident, his black stallion that he'd bought a few years ago and named after the SEAL's insignia, lifted his magnificent head, but remained cautious.

"Do you think Ella would like to see the horses?" Clint asked.

"Maybe," Bree said. "At least Frosty. I'm not sure Trident would put up with a fussy baby."

"Not to worry. Trident is so antisocial he won't even come up to the fence to say hello."

Clint stepped ahead to whistle. Frosty came running to the fence and issued a long neigh in greeting. Or perhaps he was chastising Clint for being away for so long. A tan-gray Kentucky Mountain Saddle Horse, Frosty was usually gentle and willing.

"Hey, fella." Clint rubbed Frosty's nose as the old guy whinnied his joy. "I missed you, too."

Bree moved slowly toward them. Ella's eyes grew even bigger, and when Frosty shook his head and snorted, she laughed.

"I think it's safe to come closer," Clint said.

Bree eased forward until Ella could touch Frosty's head. When he moved, her laughter rang through the air, the sound joyous and perfect.

Clint's heart melted on the spot. How wonderful it would be to have children and teach them to ride. To bring pure joy back to the ranch that had been bitter to him for so many years as a child. To bring joy to his own life. Sure, he had a good life. Liked what he did. Had a real sense of purpose. But joy? Not so much.

A horse came galloping up the driveway, and Clint moved his hand to his gun. He stepped between the rider and Bree. "Stay behind me."

When Clint could identify the horse and rider, he blew out a breath. "It's Shawn. The deputy I told you about."

Clint stepped to the side so Bree could see Shawn, but Clint didn't relax. He'd let the sweet moment with Bree and Ella distract him, and he'd let down his guard. He couldn't let that happen again.

Shawn halted his horse and slid down from the saddle to tie the reins to the fence. Clint was glad to see his longtime friend. They'd hung out since middle school and rode the rodeo circuit together in high school summers.

Shawn stepped over to them and clapped Clint on the back. "Good to see you, man."

"You too, bro." Clint introduced Bree and Ella.

Shawn lifted his hat, his full head of orangey red hair springing free, and bowed. "Nice to meet you, ma'am."

"Bree. Please." She smiled at Shawn.

He returned it wholeheartedly then slapped his hat back on his head. Single and wanting to settle down, Shawn would be the perfect man for Bree. He was a steady guy, hard worker, even tempered and kind. He was also far more like Bree in personality than Clint was.

So why was Clint already trying to come up with a way to keep them apart?

"I'm sorry to hear about your friends," Shawn said. "And sorry the detective hasn't been of more help. I can understand how a detective's heavy caseload means prioritizing where he focuses his attention, and all of your situations have been circumstantial until today."

"Nothing circumstantial about three Texas coral snakes," Clint said. "When Bree called Detective Newlin, he couldn't blow this one off."

"So he's going to investigate?"

Clint nodded. "He even sent out a forensic team, but I'm still not confident he'll make this a priority so we'll keep digging and want your help."

"You got it, man. I'm glad to use my days off to help, but remember my help is unofficial. Even if I was on duty, everything that's happened so far has been outside of my jurisdiction."

"I appreciate your willingness to help us," Bree said.

"No problem, but you should know, I'm not a detective."

"Still, you're light-years ahead of us on crime investigation techniques."

"You hear that, man?" Shawn shouldered Clint. "She already recognizes my amazing talent and skills."

Bree laughed, but Clint could only manage a strained

smile. "Let's go back to the house and work on a game plan for tomorrow."

They set off and as Bree shifted Ella, Shawn said, "If she's getting heavy, I can carry her for you."

Bree smiled up at Shawn. "That would be wonderful."

Clint stifled a grumble. Why hadn't he offered to do the same thing? Simple. He wouldn't even know how to hold Ella, where Shawn was the oldest of six kids, and he'd toted babies around for years.

Shawn settled Ella in his arms, and she immediately grabbed onto his hat.

"Whoa, little filly," he said good-naturedly. "A man and his hat are like a man and his horse. You just don't come between them."

Bree laughed, and Clint's heart warmed at the sound at the same time as jealousy settled into his stomach.

*Get a grip, man.*

"About the gouge on the boat," Clint said to draw Shawn's attention. "Now that I've seen it, I think you could get a big enough paint sample to have it analyzed like you do with cars."

"Right," Shawn said. "But you should know that boats aren't as simple as cars. People don't often repaint their cars, leaving the factory color for as long as the car's in use. It's not like that with boats. Since they're in water and need to be repainted on a regular basis we don't have a database of colors. But once we compile a list of suspects, the gouge paint can be matched against a suspect's boat for confirmation, so I'll take a sample of the paint in the morning."

"I have some boat registration numbers for you to run, too," Clint said.

"Now that I can do. Should have the owners' names for you when we meet tomorrow."

"Finally a lead." Bree smiled again.

Clint nodded his appreciation, but he wasn't going to get too excited. Who knew how many leads they'd have to check out before they found the culprit? And in the meantime, there was still a killer out there who could attack again at any moment.

# FIVE

The bright morning sun glinted off the boat as Bree watched Clint and Shawn chatting a few feet away. They both had a commanding presence but were nothing alike in appearance except in their height. Shawn was slender, had a ready smile and flaming red hair. Clint was packed with muscle, his full mouth often in a frown, and his brown hair was only remarkable when the sun caught the copper highlights as it was doing now.

Shawn pulled a folded stack of papers from his back pocket and handed the top sheet to Clint. "The boat owners. If anyone asks, you didn't get the names from me."

Clint glanced at the paper then held it out to Bree. "Recognize anyone?"

She read the names Isaac Ellison, Kier Lee and Vern Porter, each listed with local addresses.

"Never heard of them," she said.

"With today's social media and the internet," Shawn said, "you shouldn't have any trouble finding additional information on them."

Clint pocketed the list. "We can research them after we finish the boat search."

Shawn handed the other pages to Clint. "Before we get started, here's the police report from the drive-by shooting.

You can read it later, but for now you should know there are three noteworthy items. First, a witness saw a man in a white Toyota Corolla without license plates shooting at the house. Second, the shooter used a rifle, which we already suspected."

"And the third point?" Clint asked.

"Slugs recovered at the scene are .338 Lapua Magnums."

"Interesting." Clint faced Bree. "This caliber was developed for the military—specifically the Marines—for long-range sniper rifles."

"So it's only used by the military?" she asked.

"Not quite. It's not as common as other calibers but it's gaining in popularity with hunters and civilian long-range shooting enthusiasts. Still, this could help narrow down the suspect list."

"Oh, good." Bree quickly scanned the report then looked up at Clint. "What about the witness? Should we follow up with him to see if he's remembered anything else about that night?"

"I'll be glad to do that for you," Shawn offered. "But let's get to the search as it'll take time to process any evidence we find."

"Where do you want to start?" Bree asked.

"Let me see the gouge first."

Bree led him to the damaged spot. Shawn leaned over the edge of the boat to examine it. Then he grabbed his bag and took out a knife and paper envelope to scrape paint flakes into the envelope and seal it. "Let's look at the engine hatch next."

Clint stepped over to the hatch and met Bree's gaze. "You should stand back just in case."

"You don't think—"

"No. I don't think we'll find anything dangerous this time, but caution is the name of the game."

"You SEALs are such drama queens." Shawn laughed and stepped to the far end of the hatch.

Bree was surprised Clint didn't offer even a hint of a smile, but solemnly bent to the hatch. "Ready?"

Shawn nodded.

Bree held her breath as they lifted the door, but as predicted, nothing popped up or slithered out.

Once Clint secured the door in an open position, Shawn withdrew a flashlight from his duffel and lay down on his belly to peer into the space. Bree came closer to watch.

"The black powder you're seeing is from a forensic tech's fingerprint search," Shawn explained. "I'll do the same thing before we go, but looks like they were thorough and likely lifted all the viable prints."

He swept the light over the pristine engine, and then paused to stare at one spot. "I see a few drops of blood by the generator. Could be from Jason or Laura—making repairs or performing maintenance—or from the killer, if he tampered with it."

"Can it be compared to Jason's and Laura's blood type?" Bree asked.

Shawn grinned. "It certainly can. I'm a forensic wannabe, I happen to have the right equipment to grab a sample. And I've got a friend in the lab who can process it."

"You won't be risking your job if you do this, will you?" Bree asked.

"Detective Newlin has already processed the scene and released it, so I won't be contaminating evidence, and my friend can run this sample without any problem." He reached into his tote bag and brought out tape and a pencil.

Clint squatted next to him. "Tape for a bloodstain? Never seen that done before even on those CSI shows."

"Collecting blood really depends on the type of surface and quantity of blood, and if it's wet or dried. You can scrape dried bloodstains into an envelope, but they tend to break into small flakes that frequently get lost during the scraping process. Since there's so little blood, I want to collect as much of it as I can."

He placed a strip of tape over the spot then rubbed it with the pencil eraser. He then lifted the tape. "I'll put this on a vinyl acetate backing card and my friend will be good to go." Once that was done, he started checking for any missed fingerprints.

While he worked, Bree came to her feet and so did Clint. A flash of light down the dock caught Bree's attention. Before she could take a better look, Clint grabbed her shoulders and directed her inside.

"Stay in here," he warned.

Shawn looked up. "What is it?"

"Sun glinting off binoculars. A guy at the end of the dock has them trained on us."

"Do you think it's the killer?" Bree asked, her words barely louder than a whisper.

Clint wanted to go with Shawn, who'd headed down the dock to confront the observer. But there was no way Clint would leave Bree alone and exposed to danger for even a nanosecond.

He opened the door to the head. "Let's move you into the bathroom. It's on the port side so you'll be as far away from the man as possible."

She entered the small space. "Do you really think it's the killer?"

"I'm not taking any chances."

The roar of a boat engine cut through the air, covering her response.

"Stay here," Clint warned and moved to the porthole on the starboard side of the boat.

"What is it?" she asked.

"A large cabin cruiser leaving the dock. There's a big guy at the helm, but that's all I can see. Shawn's heading back this way. Hopefully he can tell us more."

Clint stepped to the cabin door and watched Shawn jog up the dock and onto the boat, which dipped and rolled with his weight.

Clint widened his stance to adjust for the movement. "I assume that was the guy with binoculars taking off in the boat."

Shawn nodded and paused to catch his breath. "I called dispatch to get someone out here to trail the boat. Unfortunately, it'll take a while for someone to arrive. And with the many public boat ramps on this lake—"

"This guy will get away," Clint interrupted in frustration.

"Correct."

"What about the guy or his boat?" Bree asked. "Did you catch any distinguishing features?"

"Boat's big. Maybe a forty footer. I only saw the guy's back. He's six feet, 220 pounds. He wore a navy baseball cap, but that's one of the Rangers' team colors, and I doubt it will help us find him."

Clint agreed that many locals would own caps from the nearest professional baseball team. "What about registration numbers on the boat?"

"By the time I got to down the dock, he was taking off so I wasn't able to catch the numbers. I did notice a wide blue stripe though. With the size of the boat, it could have done the damage on this one."

"That's something, then," Bree said, but she sounded like she didn't believe her own statement.

Clint faced her. "It'll be safer for you if we take off while this guy is still on the run."

"If you leave a key," Shawn said, "I can finish my search and lock up before taking the blood and any other evidence I find to the lab."

Bree dug the key ring from her pocket and snapped off a key. "Thank you for your help. I hope I can repay you someday."

"I don't need repayment, but if you're not seeing anyone..." He winked.

Clint eyed Shawn. "We need to go now."

"Hey, man, I was just joking around."

"Not a good idea to waste time with jokes when a killer is out there." Clint tried not to snap, but he didn't manage it. "I'd like you to walk the path to my truck then call me if we're clear to leave."

Shawn nodded and held up the key. "I'll get this back to you tonight."

He stepped off, and Clint faced Bree.

"You were kind of hard on him," she said.

Clint ran a hand around the back of his neck and rubbed stiff muscles. "I'll apologize when we get to my truck."

She eyed him, but didn't say another word. It wasn't hard to see his terse attitude disappointed her. In truth, he was disappointed with himself. Shawn was simply trying to help. Plus, he was a true friend and wouldn't hit on her for real.

Clint's phone rang and, seeing Shawn's name, he answered.

"You're clear," Shawn said.

"Hey, man. Sorry I snapped at you."

"My fault, bro. I can see that you still have a thing for Bree. I shouldn't joke about dating her."

"Roger that," Clint said to keep from giving even a hint

to Bree about what they were discussing. He disconnected. "We're clear to leave."

He stepped onto the deck and ran his gaze over the dock. Sure, Shawn had cleared the area, but as a SEAL, Clint knew things could change and lives could be lost in a heartbeat.

# SIX

Bree stepped through the door of Laura and Jason's small ranch house. She paused in the family room entrance. Memories assaulted her. Memories of decorating the place with Laura, parties in the family room, barbecues on the large deck, and frequent afternoons when she and Laura popped popcorn and watched chick flicks or just talked about their lives while Jason went golfing.

Then there was the day Laura brought Ella home to the nursery Bree had helped decorate. Oh, the joy. Indescribable for Jason and Laura, and for Bree who served as Ella's godmother. Never did she imagine she'd have to fulfill her promise to step in and become Ella's mother.

An involuntary cry of anguish escaped, and she clamped a hand over her mouth as tears ran down her cheeks.

Clint came up behind her. "I should have realized how hard this would be for you. I could have come over here alone."

She shook her head, but she couldn't form a word in response.

"It's okay, honey." He turned her into his arms. "I'm here for you. Go ahead and cry it out again."

He was right. He was here for her. For now, but he wouldn't be here for long. His leave would end, and he'd go back to risking his life on dangerous missions. She didn't want that. Not at all. Her crying ramped up.

"Shh," he kept whispering as he patted her back.

She should pull away before she became too dependent on him, but she clung tightly and let the tears fall. When she could cry no more, she leaned back and looked up at him. His eyes were soft with compassion. Marveling at the depth of caring in his expression, she brushed her fingers over his cheek.

"Thank you," she whispered as she lost herself in his eyes.

He started to speak, then stopped and cleared his throat. "We were always good together, weren't we?"

"Yes," she whispered, letting her hand drift to the spot on his shirt dampened by her tears. "It was the apart that I couldn't handle. I still can't handle it."

"And I can't change jobs." The emotion had left his voice, leaving a flat, disappointed tone.

She drew back. "And that leaves us in the same place."

He didn't seem like he wanted to agree, but he nodded. "And if it's possible, I hate it even more that we'll have to go our separate ways when this is all over."

Sadness and disappointment drew her toward him to nestle in his arms and take comfort, but she resisted. Clinging to him would only increase the urge to have him in her life.

She pushed from his arms. "We should try to limit the time we spend alone together, and it'll be easier."

"Maybe," he said, but he didn't seem to believe it. He gestured at a desk in the corner holding Jason's laptop. "The computer should be a great place to find work information. At least if it's not password-protected."

"As usual, Jason thought of everything. In the paperwork that came with the will, he left detailed instructions on how to access his laptop so I could locate information about his accounts." She crossed the room, sat in the leather chair and booted up the computer where she entered the password she'd committed to memory.

Clint came to stand behind her. "Email's a good place to start."

She forced her attention to the screen and clicked on the email icon. A window opened displaying two profiles. One was labeled work and the other home.

"Start with work," Clint suggested.

She opened the account and clicked on the last email received before Jason died. The message was from an Isaac Ellison.

"That's one of the names Shawn gave us," Clint said.

The email referenced an insurance issue with Jason's client. There was no mention of the client's name, just an account number, but Isaac demanded to talk to Jason about the client.

Clint pointed at the email signature. "Looks like Isaac was Jason's boss, and he doesn't sound very happy with Jason."

Bree peered up at Clint. "If work spilled into their personal lives, he could also be the guy who argued with Jason at the marina. And from there it could have escalated to murder."

Isaac Ellison led Bree and Clint down the hall toward his office located in the outskirts of McKinney. Bree mimed for Clint that Isaac was of the right physical build to be the man who'd fled from the marina earlier that day. Clint nodded his understanding and agreement.

Isaac stepped into the small space and gestured at chairs sitting in front of his desk. Bree took a seat and ran her gaze over the room. The office was nondescript except for boating pictures on the wall. Bree didn't know much about boats, but it was obvious that the cabin cruiser in the pictures matched the one they saw in the marina that could have damaged Jason's boat.

"Nice boat," she said. "Is it yours?"

"Yes." He frowned. "Jason and I were good friends. We often went boating together. I still can't believe he's gone."

She hadn't seen this man at Jason's funeral, much less heard Laura or Jason mention him, so she doubted they were *good* friends. Was the man simply exaggerating—or was he outright lying?

"I'm not convinced that Jason would be careless enough to die from carbon monoxide poisoning," she said.

"I found that odd, too. I know he was careful not to run his AC at night."

*Interesting.* "Did you tell the police that?"

He shook his head. "I figured it was just too hot that night, and he decided to risk running it."

"If his death wasn't an accident," Clint said, "can you think of anyone who might have wanted to kill Jason or Laura?"

Isaac shook his head.

"Maybe Jason had a disgruntled client," Bree suggested as she and Clint had decided not to tell Isaac that they'd read the email and to wait for him to offer information.

"Not that I know of, and I gotta think that if someone was angry enough to attack Jason over one of his decisions, that Jason would have told me about it."

"What exactly did Jason's job as an adjuster entail?" Clint asked.

"He reviewed insurance claims and either approved or denied them."

"So he could have made someone mad by denying their claim."

"Sure, happens all the time, but mad enough to kill? Nah. I can't see that."

"Would you mind checking his case files just in case he failed to mention an extremely upset client to you?" Bree asked.

"Sure, yeah. I'm glad to take a look, but he had a heavy caseload so it'll take some time."

He was going out of his way to seem helpful and agreeable, but after reading his email to Jason, Bree suspected it was a front. She doubted he'd follow through and actually contact her about any clients and they'd have to question him again about the email.

"Have you been here all day?" Clint asked.

"Yeah, why?"

Clint shrugged. "What about the night Jason died? Where were you then?"

Isaac's eyes narrowed. "Not that it's any of your business, but I was home with my wife."

"One of the marina workers told us they saw Jason arguing with a man of your size and build on the dock just before he died," Bree said. "Could that have been you?"

Isaac's narrow lips dipped in a frown. "Wasn't me."

"You're sure?" Clint asked, and Bree knew he doubted Isaac just as she did.

"Positive." He glanced at his watch then stood. "I'm swamped this afternoon. I'll walk you out."

He rushed them out the door and to the exit.

At the elevator to street level, Bree peered up at Clint. "He sure was in a hurry to get rid of us."

"Agreed."

She boarded the elevator. "I'm thinking he was the guy who argued with Jason. And the guy who was watching us earlier today."

"I don't know about that, but I don't think he was completely truthful with us."

"Maybe we should have asked him about the email."

Clint shook his head. "I still think it was best to wait. We don't want to scare him into destroying any evidence."

When the door opened on ground level, Clint's gaze turned razor-sharp, and his arm went around her waist to snug her tight against his side. She didn't know if he'd seen something suspicious or if he was just being cautious, but she gladly accepted his protection and stayed close until she climbed into his truck.

He sat behind the wheel and she swiveled to face him. "Do you think we should go back to the marina and question the woman who saw Jason's argument?"

"It wouldn't hurt." Clint stared ahead.

"What are you thinking?"

He peered at her. "That Jason's death is work-related, and Isaac knows about it, but isn't going to admit it, and that we have our work cut out for us."

"Knows about it…as in, he knows who did it? So you don't think he's the killer himself?"

"Not necessarily. He got flustered toward the end, when we had him talk about his whereabouts. He wasn't expecting those questions. But he was calm and collected when it came to talking about Jason's angry clients—as if he'd practiced saying that part and had planned his answers."

"But if he wasn't involved in the murders, why lie about the clients? Why not just tell the authorities about whoever had a grudge against Jason?"

"I didn't say he wasn't involved," Clint replied. "I just think this might have been something more complicated than a simple denied claim. Maybe there were other factors involved—bribes or payouts of some kind. Or maybe there was some kind of deal or scam that went wrong."

"Are you suggesting Jason was involved in something unethical or illegal?"

"Maybe."

"No. If you knew Jason, you'd know that wasn't possible. He was a man of faith and principles. He'd never do anything unscrupulous."

"You'd be surprised what good people are capable of doing," he replied.

"Not Jason."

She turned away and caught sight of Isaac rushing out of the building. "Look."

Clint swiveled. "So much for being swamped."

Isaac climbed into a white SUV and roared past them.

"Do you think our visit spooked him?"

"Let's follow him and find out." Clint started the truck and eased into traffic.

He hung back, and Bree kept her gaze fixed on Isaac's SUV until he turned into the marina parking lot.

Clint pulled to the side of the road. "We'll give him a chance to park and get out of his car so he doesn't see us."

Bree wanted to race after Isaac, but Clint had experience in evasion tactics so she tried to be patient. Clint finally eased forward, and Bree saw Isaac starting down the gangway toward the slips.

Clint parked near Isaac's SUV. "I don't like the idea of you getting out of the truck here, but I like leaving you behind even less. So stay next to me and follow my directions."

Bree nodded and, by the time she stepped down from the truck, he'd jogged to her door. She expected his arm would settle at her waist, and once it did, they moved at a quick clip, trailing Isaac into the maze of boats.

"He's boarding his boat." As she spoke, he ducked into the cabin.

"If he's in the cabin, he's not leaving the dock."

"Maybe he has something onboard that he needs to get."

Clint picked up speed. "I'm going straight inside. You stay behind me. Move softly to keep from alerting him."

He stepped onto the platform then helped her board. Holding her hand now, he quickly led her toward the cabin door.

"Stop!" he shouted at the cabin door, apparently having seen something that made him discard his stealthy approach. He dropped her hand and rushed forward.

Bree entered behind him and saw papers burning in the stainless steel sink. Isaac held a trash can over the sink as if he planned to add the items in the can to the flames.

Clint knocked the can from Isaac's hand. She thought he might wrestle Isaac to the ground to stop him, but he stood glaring at Isaac instead.

"You have no right to be on my boat," Isaac snapped. "Get off now."

"We just want to talk."

"Is that so?" Isaac's breath came hard and fast. "Is that why you're trespassing and assaulting me?"

"Trust me," Clint said. "If I'd assaulted you, you wouldn't be standing upright."

"Well you're certainly trespassing." Isaac dug out his phone from his pocket. "And if you don't leave, I'll call the police."

Clint raised his hands. "Relax. We're going."

He backed toward Bree, but stopped by the trash can. "What's with the bloody tissues in the trash?"

"I get frequent nosebleeds."

Clint didn't respond, but Bree could tell he wanted to say something. Instead, he gestured for her to step out first. Outside the cabin, he took her hand again.

"Did you believe the nosebleed comment?" she asked.

"Yeah."

"But why?"

"He came up with the answer too fast for it to be a lie. And if he'd hurt himself on Jason's boat he'd have emptied his trash a long time ago."

"But you looked like you wanted to say something else."

"Say something? Nah. I thought about grabbing a tissue for Shawn to compare to the blood found on Jason's boat."

"Why didn't you?"

"He was watching us—he could have accused us of theft. Anyway, if what he says is true about frequent nose-bleeds, we'll have a chance to collect a bloody tissue in the future."

"The future," she mumbled. "Sounds like you don't think this will be resolved anytime soon."

He met her gaze and held it. "I'm sorry, Bree. But I don't. We may have a few leads, but it's going to take time to track them down, leaving you in danger for far longer than I'd hoped."

# SEVEN

Back at the ranch, Clint sat at the kitchen table while Bree and her mother prepared dinner. He loved seeing them work together in such harmony. His parents were like that, too. They didn't need to communicate but knew each other's thoughts. It had once been that way with him and Bree, in tune with one another from the start. He hoped he'd be able to find that with someone else once he was finally ready to settle down. But could he really be so compatible with anyone else?

*Leave it alone. Move on. Focus on the laptop.* He opened an internet browser and typed in "Kier Lee." A link declaring him a plaintive in a malpractice lawsuit came up. Clint opened the article and read the details.

He looked up at Bree. "What's Laura's maiden name?"

"Tichler, why?"

"Ten years ago Kier Lee sued her for malpractice."

Bree's eyebrows shot up. "She never mentioned being sued."

"The newspaper story says he believed she'd given his father the wrong medicine dose and he died. She was cleared, though."

"Of course she was." Bree crossed over to him and swiveled the computer toward her.

"Even after the trial, he maintained that she was guilty," she said, her gaze not leaving the article. "Maybe he wanted to get back at her."

"But why wait ten years?"

"We need to investigate and find out."

Clint nodded. "We'll go see him in the morning. For now, I'll do some checking on Vern Porter."

Bree frowned. "I wonder why she never told me about it."

"It probably traumatized her and since she was cleared there was no point in mentioning it."

"Explains why she was always adamant that I keep my malpractice insurance up to date."

Crying sounded from the master bedroom and Bree looked like she wanted to sigh but took a deep breath instead. "Excuse me."

After she left the room, Clint typed "Vern Porter" into the computer, and a long list of links populated the screen. Clicking through one by one, Clint discovered Porter owned a gun range in the area and was quoted in several articles on game hunting.

The guy obviously knew his way around weapons, and would be a good candidate for owning the gun used to shoot up Bree's house. Clint continued to search but couldn't find any obvious link between Porter and Jason or Laura, but that didn't mean it wasn't there. He was seeming just as likely a suspect as Lee, and they needed to talk to him in the morning as well.

Bree returned with Ella. The baby's eyes were red and puffy and her face a blotchy red as she cried out in pain. "I couldn't find the teething gel."

"I think it's on the table in the family room," Marie replied.

Since Marie was up to her arms in soapy water at the sink, Clint jumped up. "I'll get it."

He quickly found the gel and brought it to Bree.

"Can you hold Ella for a minute so I can wash my hands?" she asked.

"Me?"

"She won't break."

"But won't it upset her more?"

Bree didn't respond but simply held Ella out. Clint wasn't sure what to do, but he mimicked the way Bree had held the baby. He got a firm grip and nestled her close to his chest.

"Shh, honey," he said, doing the only thing he could think of.

She stopped crying for a moment and hiccupped while she stared at him.

"That's better." He made a goofy face at her.

He saw the beginnings of a smile so he made an even funnier face. Her smile widened.

"She likes you," Marie said.

Bree turned from the sink. "She hasn't been around men much since Jason died, and she always got on well with men."

Clint didn't care if Ella liked other men. She was responding to him, and his heart melted in a giant puddle. He'd known he wanted to have children, but now—now, with this sweet little face looking up at him... Man. He really wanted a family. Starting with a wife, of course.

Ella patted chubby hands on his face and quickly pulled them back, looking displeased.

"Don't like my whiskers, huh?" He chuckled, and she grinned, seeming to have forgotten all about her pain.

"Maybe you should take her into the family room while Bree and I finish making dinner," Marie suggested.

"If you want to, of course," Bree added.

"Sure. Why not?" His words came out sounding bold, but his innards were still quaking with fear over caring for this petite person.

He took a seat and settled Ella on his lap facing him then patted her hands together as he'd seen Bree do. Ella rewarded him with another toothless smile. She was cute now, but he imagined she'd be adorable when her first tooth broke through.

How long would that take? Would he even see her when it did?

He had no clue, but he'd like to see it.

*Is this You, God? Trying to tell me something here?*

But what was he supposed to learn from this and why now?

*You put the call in my heart for the SEALs, and as far as I can see, You haven't released me from that call.*

Ella's chin wobbled, and her lower lip poked out. He expected her to wail at any moment so he started patting her hands again. Her lip went back in and soon he had her grinning and laughing.

Bree stepped into the room. "You two seem to be getting along just fine."

"We are."

She crossed the space to sit on the arm of the sofa and stroked her hand over Ella's head. "You like Clint, don't you, precious?"

Her grin widened, and Clint peered up at Bree. Love flowed from her very expressive eyes, and it was easy to imagine holding their child, or even this sweetheart, as they raised her together. Way too easy to picture it.

"I forgot there's something I have to do." He quickly handed Ella back to Bree and rushed through the kitchen, grabbing a peppermint treat for Frosty on the way to the back door.

"Dinner will be ready in a few minutes," Marie said.

"Thanks, but I've lost my appetite."

He hurried across the yard toward the corral where Pete leaned against the rail, a piece of straw sticking from his mouth.

*Coward,* Clint told himself. *Running from Bree and Ella, everything you want, instead of facing things head-on like you've been taught.*

"Yeah, well, sometimes you have to run before you do something that you know isn't good for you or the other person," he mumbled.

"You say something?" Pete asked.

"Not anything I want anyone else to hear," Clint said. "For that matter, I don't much want to hear it myself."

Bree finished loading the dishwasher while glancing at the door every few minutes as she'd done since Clint rushed outside and didn't return. Something she'd said or done had made him take off, and she wanted to talk to him about it.

She closed the dishwasher and listened to the water rush in. She'd already put Ella down for the night, and she had no reason not to go looking for him. She poked her head into the family room where her mom sat reading in an overstuffed arm chair.

"Can you keep an ear out for Ella? I'm going to see if I can find Clint."

She frowned. "You're not getting attached to him again, are you?"

"No," Bree replied without thinking. "Is it okay for me to go?"

"Sure, but sweetie." She met and held Bree's gaze. "As

far as I can see, Clint isn't leaving the SEALS, and if you don't take care, you're going to end up with a broken heart again."

"I'm fine, Mom." She spun and grabbed a granola bar for Clint since he'd missed dinner, then stepped outside.

Her gaze went to the millions of stars sparkling overhead, reminding her of dinners with Clint on the patio. They'd sat in comfy chairs, gazed up at a glittering sky and talked about their dreams for hours at a time. Until one day they discovered their dreams could never be realized together.

"Remember that," she warned herself as she headed for the barn where light spilled through the windows.

She found Clint sitting on a turned-over pail in Frosty's stall. He held a metal pick in one hand, and Frosty's foot in the other. He looked up. "Just cleaning out his hooves."

She held up the granola bar. He shrugged off his leather gloves and took it. "Thanks."

"We missed you at dinner."

"I had some thinking to do. Ella doing okay?" He unwrapped the bar and chomped off a third of it in one bite.

"She's fast asleep. For how long, I don't know, but she's quiet for now." Bree stepped over to Frosty and petted his velvety soft head. "Hey, fella."

She glanced at Clint who was studying her as he took another big bite of the bar.

"I'm glad to see Frosty still looking so well at his age," she said.

"This old guy?" Clint got up and joined her. "He's gonna be around for a long time to come, aren't you, bud?"

Frosty tossed back his head and whinnied as if he understood.

"Do you still ride him?" she asked.

Clint nodded as he finished chewing the last of his bar

and shoved the wrapper in his pocket. "I have to be careful with him, though. Senior horses have a problem regulating their temperature. So I keep an eye on his breathing to tell me if he's overheating."

"Sounds like you know a lot about horses."

"I lost my parents. I wasn't about to lose the horse they gave me our last Christmas together. So I learned everything I could about them. It also gave me something to do when Granddad basically ignored me."

"I don't know how he could do that."

"He always grumbled about having to leave the military to take care of me, but I think his real problem with me was that seeing me around here reminded him of my dad dying."

"I still don't get it. Every time I look at Ella, I'm reminded of Laura and Jason, but that makes me want to love her even more."

"That's who you are. Granddad was just a gruff old guy with no clue how to show affection."

"I'm glad you're not like that."

"No?"

She shook her head emphatically.

"Guess I owe that to my faith. Granddad was a believer, but he didn't live his faith. I was fortunate to learn from my parents before they died."

"And now you're using your faith to make the world a better place."

"I'd like to hope I am." He stroked Frosty's mane, but stared into the distance. "Sitting out here, cleaning hooves, I'm reminded of how much I love the simple life on the ranch."

"Maybe you could come back permanently," she said hopefully then shook her head. "I'm sorry, that's not fair.

Just because I want you to come back doesn't mean it's right for you. I'm being selfish."

He released Frosty and took her hand. "You know there's a part of me that wants to be here, right? With you?"

"I've been getting that feeling," she said, hoping that he might be open to finally making the change.

"I'm not trying to lead you on."

Hope dimmed. If he was worried about leading her on, that meant that he still had no intention of leaving the SEALs. "I know."

He let go of her hand and shoved his hand into his pocket. "Who knows? Maybe this wishful thinking is just because my life is so crazy away from here, and I need solitude every now and then."

"Do you usually feel this way when you come home?"

"Not really."

"But if you did come home to stay, you'd probably go stir-crazy in the simple, country life, living out here all alone."

"Probably, but if I lived here full-time, I would hope I wouldn't be alone for long." He stepped closer and slid his fingers into her hair to cup the back of her head.

"We shouldn't," she said on a breathless wave.

"I don't care about 'should' right now." He lowered his head, his lips inches from her mouth. "I want to kiss you, and I'm going to unless you tell me to stop."

She opened her mouth to speak, but the words wouldn't come out. Instead, she closed her eyes and held her breath. When his lips touched hers they set off fireworks of emotions blazing through her body.

She'd forgotten how wonderful kissing him felt. She'd never experienced anything like it and knew nothing else would ever take its place. They were meant to be together…and yet…they weren't. Her mother's warning came rushing back like ice water in her veins.

She pushed back. "I'm sorry, I can't do this."

She hurried out of the barn before she gave in to feelings that weren't in her best interest. She ran across the grounds, each step in the peaceful landscape reminding her that she'd come to enjoy the solitude of the ranch. She would love to be able to leave her job and be a full-time mother to Ella while living in such a tranquil setting.

"A pipe dream," she whispered and charged into the house.

She didn't have a man in her life to support them. At least not a man who was free to return her feelings.

# EIGHT

As the sun beat down on the parking lot, Clint heard gunshots ringing through the air at Vern Porter's firing range. A run-down place with indoor and outdoor lanes, it stood on a lot filled with older-model trucks that had seen better days—as had the building itself.

Clint held the door for Bree to step inside where shelves were loaded with ammo and weapons. Vern stood behind the counter and eyed them. His skin was leathered and tan as if he spent a good deal of time outdoors. He had piercing blue eyes and a salt-and-pepper beard.

All in all, he looked like the kind of guy you wouldn't want to encounter in a dark alley and definitely not the kind of guy to own a luxury boat. But, he *was* of the right height and build to be the guy who was spying on them at the marina and the man who'd argued with Jason.

Clint pulled Bree closer, stepped up to the counter and introduced himself. "I was wondering if you know Laura and Jason Kahn."

"Seems like I heard the names, but not sure where."

"They docked their boat near your slip."

"They the ones who died from carbon monoxide? Not a real bright idea to run a generator while sleeping."

Bree lifted her chin and seemed like she wanted to

deck the guy. "It's looking like someone tampered with their generator."

"Is that right?"

"Yes, and when I started to look into it, someone shot up my house." She eased away from Clint and planted her feet.

"And you think I might know who that someone is?"

"No, I think that someone is you." She met the guy's gaze and didn't back down.

Clint made a mental note not to make Bree mad, as she was fierce when it came to protecting her friends.

"Lookie here, missy." Vern glared at Bree.

She didn't back down, and Clint was so proud of her strength even as he worried about her recklessness, challenging this man so openly.

Vern planted his hands on the countertop. "You don't come into my place and accuse me of a crime unless you have some proof. So lay it out for me or step off."

Clint eased closer to draw Vern's attention. "Where were you on the night they died?"

"Again, once you prove you have a valid reason for asking, I'll tell you. Until then…"

"You do own a boat and dock it at the marina, though," Bree stated.

Vern blew out a breath and came to his full height. "None of your business. Now take off. I've got work to do."

"I have no choice but to believe your unwillingness to answer means you're hiding something," Bree said. "And you should know, whatever it is, we'll find out."

"Right. Like you even have the skills to find your way out of a paper bag." He marched out from behind the counter and went to open the door.

Clint moved Bree away from Vern and they stepped outside.

"Good riddance," Vern muttered.

Clint hurried Bree to his truck and settled her inside before he ran around the front.

She faced him. "What did you make of that?"

"My gut says he's a guy who likes his privacy and doesn't like anyone digging into his life."

"But you don't think he's the killer?"

"I didn't get that vibe, but I did see a Desert Tech SRS rifle locked up in the cabinet behind the counter. It's chambered for .338 Lapua Magnums so he could be our shooter. I'll have Shawn do a background check to see if he can find a connection between him and Laura or Jason to see if there's a motive to want to kill them."

"And until then?"

"We know Kier is connected to Laura, and he has a strong motive so we move on to him. Plus his boat was damaged. Let me call his office to see if we can meet with him." Clint made the call only to learn Kier had gone boating. Clint hung up and relayed the information to Bree then set out for the marina, where he kept his gaze moving over the area as he escorted Bree down the dock.

The restaurant door opened, and a tall man with dark, frizzy hair and a perfectly white smile stepped out with three other men. They were all dressed in shorts, polo shirts and boating shoes, but Clint recognized Kier from his pictures.

"The guy in the white shirt is Kier," Clint said to Bree. "We should approach him before they go out on the lake." Clint made firm eye contact with her. "Stay close to me. If I catch even a hint of danger, we're out of here."

She nodded. Convinced she'd follow his lead, he stepped up to Kier.

"Mr. Lee," Clint said loud enough to be heard over their laughter.

Kier spun and sized Clint up with a quick once-over.

"Might we have a word with you?" Clint asked.

He eyed them both, then shrugged and turned back to his friends. "I'll catch up with you."

After the men departed Clint explained their purpose. "Your boat is a perfect size and color to have damaged the Kahns' boat and you have a large scratch on your bow."

Kier's forehead scrunched. "I don't even know these people. Why would I have rammed my boat into them?"

"You sued Laura for malpractice." Bree eyed him.

Clint wasn't surprised when Kier seemed to wither under her glare. "I sued a Laura Tichler."

"Tichler is Laura Kahn's maiden name."

"Okay, so? Obviously I didn't know her married name. And obviously that means I wouldn't go ramming her boat."

"Then you wouldn't mind telling us where you were the night they died," Clint said.

Kier crossed his arms and glanced down the dock where his friends stood watching. "Actually, I do mind. My friends are waiting."

"That's not acceptable," Bree said. "This is way more important than having fun with your buddies. My friends have died and they left a baby who deserves to know the truth about their deaths when she gets older."

"I'm not the person who can shed light on that for you."

"But you *can* tell us where you were that night and how your boat got damaged so we can rule you out. We aren't leaving until you do."

"My whereabouts and my boat are none of your business."

"But if you didn't do it then—"

"Good day." He spun and strode away.

"Well that's strike number two, and it's not even noon," Bree muttered.

Clint wished he could force the guy to give them the answers they needed, but he'd have to settle for Shawn doing a background check on the guy.

He dug his phone from his pocket and dialed his friend. "I need you to look into Kier Lee. He sued Laura ten years ago for malpractice. We just talked to him, and he refused to tell us his whereabouts on the night of the Kahns' deaths or how he damaged his boat."

"I'll check him out."

"And Vern Porter, too. I really think he's just a belligerent old coot, but I saw a Desert Tech SRS at his place so you never know."

"Will do, and since I've got you on the phone, you should know that the blood we recovered from the hatch doesn't match Laura's or Jason's blood type."

"So maybe the killer tampered with the generator and cut himself."

"But wouldn't there have been blood on the generator then?"

"He could have cut himself on a tool that he took with him," Clint replied. "Or I saw bloody tissues on Isaac's boat. He said he suffered from reoccurring nosebleeds. He could have had a bleed on the boat."

"That's possible. Likely even, that a few drops would fall before he stemmed the flow with a tissue. We'll need a warrant to get a sample, though, and we haven't found anything that would allow me to request an official investigation."

"Then we need to keep digging until we do."

Clint opened the passenger door of his truck, and Bree worked hard to curtail her disappointment over failing to learn anything new from Kier or Vern.

*Please let us catch a break soon,* she prayed as Clint stepped back to give her access to the truck.

A gunshot sounded in the air and something whizzed in front of Bree, shattering the truck window.

"Gunshot," she managed to get out before Clint grabbed her and hurled them toward the ground. He took the brunt of the fall on his shoulder and held her securely as he rolled closer to the front of the truck.

"We're going to move out of the shooter's sight when I tell you," he said, his back to the gunman as he curled himself around her to protect her.

Another shot zipped overhead.

"Now! Go!"

He came to his feet swiftly and jerked her up, too, scurrying them around the front where he drew her to the ground again. A shot sounded and a bullet pinged into the truck in the location they'd just vacated.

Bree's heart refused to beat.

"Stay here," Clint commanded as he headed for the far side of the truck.

"Where are you going?" she cried out.

"To get my rifle from the cab."

"But he'll hit you."

"No he won't." His tone held such confidence that she almost believed he'd be safe. He scooted around to the driver's side.

She crept along behind to watch him. He opened the door. She heard another shot, this one aimed at the door, but he managed to dodge it as he came up, grabbed the gun from the rack in the window, then dropped back down. He duckwalked to the rear of his truck, put the rifle to his shoulder to fire, then jerked back and flattened his body against the pickup.

His gaze landed on her. "Move back to the front of the truck."

Fear for his safety froze her in place.

"Now, Bree! I can't worry about you and the shooter at the same time."

Afraid she'd distract him, she backed away and leaned against the dusty chrome bumper. She held her breath as she waited for another shot.

"Just so you know, I'm calling 911," he said.

She should have thought to do that. She'd had enough clarity to do so at her house, but she could hardly think straight now. Maybe because she knew he would take care of her. But that was a dangerous thing to count on. She shouldn't come to depend on him.

"Shots are coming from the north," he said into his phone. "I have a rifle and am hunkered down on the east side of my truck. I'll put down my rifle when your deputies arrive, but make sure they're clear that I'm not the gunman."

Time ticked slowly by. She held her body rigid, waiting for, but praying against, another shot. She wanted the shooter caught, but she also hoped he'd taken off without firing another round so Clint wouldn't get hurt. When sirens sounded in the distance, she sagged against the bumper. Clint joined her and called Shawn to ask him to come to the scene. After Clint hung up, he faced her.

He ran his gaze over her. "Are you okay? Nothing injured?"

"I'm good," she said but she was a mess inside and her hands trembled. She'd almost lost her life, for crying out loud. That bullet had been close. Way too close.

Patrol cars came screaming into the parking lot and chaos reigned while the deputies sorted things out. They kept Bree and Clint sitting by the truck to take their statements and didn't let them get up until Shawn arrived to vouch for them. When Bree stood, her legs threatened to buckle and she planted a hand on the hood to stay upright.

Shawn tossed his keys to Clint. "Forensics will need to retrieve slugs from your truck. Go ahead and take mine back to the ranch, and I'll bring yours by as soon as I know anything."

"Thank you, Shawn." Bree forced out a smile. "You've been so helpful."

"No need to thank me." Shawn peered at Clint. "Be careful leaving here."

Clint gave a firm nod, but the fact that a warning needed to be issued raised Bree's concern. The moment she climbed into the truck and Clint left her to run around the front, her apprehension escalated. As it continued to do until Clint got them on the road.

Instead of counting on Clint's protection alone, she kept her gaze moving along the roadside and tried to ignore her continued agitation. By the time they reached the ranch, her adrenaline had ebbed, fatigue set in, and she could barely walk toward the house. Her mom and Ella were napping so Bree took the opportunity to rest, too. When she woke, she heard Shawn and Clint in conversation, and she hurried to join them in the family room.

She took a seat on the sofa next to Shawn. "What did I miss?"

Clint shifted in the arm chair. "Slugs recovered from my truck matched the caliber from the drive-by shooting."

"So it's likely the same shooter, then."

Shawn nodded. "Also, during the forensic search a scrap of fabric from a wet suit was found on a screw near the boat's gouge. Do you know if Laura or Jason owned wet suits?"

She shook her head. "They weren't into water sports except boating. Maybe the killer swam up to the boat."

"Maybe." Clint rested his elbows on his knees. "Or maybe the killer wore a wet suit to try to minimize leaving evidence behind."

"It's possible, I suppose, that the killer bought a suit for that reason alone," Shawn said. "But it would still be a good idea to look at our suspects to see if any of them were into other water sports."

"I saw wet suits on Isaac's boat, but we'll need to check on the other guys," Clint said.

"Detective Newlin is already on that."

"Will he keep you informed?" Bree asked.

Shawn shrugged. "Detectives tend to keep things close to the vest in a murder investigation."

"So now even the police agree that it was murder," Bree mumbled. "I didn't think Laura and Jason died by accident, but the word murder just sounds so horrible."

Clint worked the muscle in his jaw. "I'm going to question all three suspects again in the morning."

"You should probably leave this up to Newlin," Shawn suggested.

"No." Clint came to his feet. "Not after the shooter nearly took both of us out today. I'm going to find the guy and make sure he pays."

Bree opened her mouth to respond, but Ella's cries sounded from the bedroom.

"Excuse me," she said expecting the men to keep talking, but they were silent as she stepped from the room.

Once she'd changed Ella, Bree fixed the little sweetheart's bottle then settled in a rocker in the bedroom. Ella readily took the bottle, hopefully a sign that her teething pain had lessened. Bree leaned back and stared into the distance, her mind racing with everything that had happened.

She wanted to be strong—had to be strong for Ella—but now that she was alone, she couldn't contain her fear.

Her life was on the line. So was Clint's. Her mother and Ella could be in danger, too. Sure, Clint took extra precautions to be sure no one followed them to the ranch, but he'd also admitted that it wasn't impossible for the killer to know their location.

"What's to become of us?" she said to Ella. To the walls. To no one. "We're in a bad situation right now, and even when it's over, I don't know if I can raise you the way your mom and dad wanted."

"Oh, sweetheart, stop," her mom said from the doorway. She crossed the room to kneel by Bree. "You have to quit worrying about that or you'll make yourself crazy."

"If only I could."

"If there's one thing I've learned in life, it's that peace can't coexist with worry. It's impossible. You have let go of the worry. If not for your own well-being, do it for Ella before she picks up on it."

"With everything going on, how can I not be worried?"

"God promises to take care of us if we trust Him and don't try to take things into our own hands."

"Easy to say when your life isn't messed up, but now?" She shook her head. "First I lose Laura and Jason without any warning. Now my life and everyone around me is in danger. How do you find peace in all of that?"

"You can start by recognizing God is protecting you."

"Is He protecting me? Is He really?"

Her mom watched her, but what she was searching for, Bree had no idea. Maybe she was simply disappointed in Bree's lack of faith. She took Bree's hand, the warmth helping chase out some of her concern.

"There's a reason Clint's in your life again." Her mom

made strong eye contact. "I see it as God providing protection for us when we need it."

"Maybe," Bree said, and knew the thought was bound to keep her tossing and turning all night as she tried to work out God's plan here. If she wasn't already awake because a killer had nearly ended her life today.

# NINE

Ella had woken crying in the morning, and they'd tried everything to console her to no avail. Clint wanted to do something to help her, but the best way to help was to find the guy trying to kill Bree so she could put her full focus on Ella.

"I'm going to try rocking her," Bree said and stepped out of the kitchen.

Marie peered at Clint across the breakfast table. "Are you ready to take off?"

He nodded.

"I think it would be a good idea if Bree stayed here with Ella today."

He watched Marie for a moment, looking for any ulterior motives. "There's a killer targeting Bree, and I don't want her out of my sight."

"There's been no sign of the killer knowing our location."

"True," Clint replied, but he wouldn't back down.

She cleared her throat. "I also think it would be good for you to take some time away from each other."

At her tone, Clint lifted his chin. "Why's that?"

"Relax," she said. "I don't have anything against you. It's just that you've been thrown together almost twenty-four/seven, and a break might help you both get a handle on what's going on between you."

"I—"

Marie held up her hands. "Don't try to deny that you have feelings for each other. It's way too obvious, and I hope you figure out a way to be together."

Clint's mouth fell open. He knew Bree had been hurt when they'd broken up. He'd have expected Marie to hate him, yet she wanted Clint to work things out with Bree.

"She really cares about you, and I want her to be happy," Marie said as if reading his mind.

"I care about her, too, so you should understand why I won't leave her here."

Marie sat up straighter. "Couldn't Shawn come over?"

"He's going with me to question the suspects."

"Then maybe his department could provide another deputy."

It didn't take a rocket scientist to see she wasn't going to back down, and she was right. He could use some time to figure out his feelings for Bree, and maybe she could use a break from being with him all the time, too. And as Marie also said, the killer had shown no signs of knowing about the ranch.

"I'll give Shawn a call and see what we can do."

She squeezed his hand. "Thank you, Clint."

He nodded and dialed Shawn who gladly arranged for a fellow deputy to spend the day at the ranch. An hour later, Ella was still fussing when Deputy Ron Broom knocked on the front door.

Clint let him in, introduced him to Bree and then led her to the far side of the room. He forced back his unease over leaving her at the ranch and smiled. "I'm only a phone call away if you need me."

"Don't worry, we'll be fine."

Clint rested a hand on her shoulder, but he needed more.

He bent down and kissed her cheek and didn't care if anyone was watching them. "Stay safe, honey."

She suddenly reached up and grabbed him in a hug. "You and Shawn watch your backs, too."

He held her close for a moment then released her. At the door, he stopped and eyed Broom. "Don't make me regret leaving them in your care."

"No, sir," Broom replied.

"Lock the door behind me." Clint stepped outside and waited to hear the snick of the deadbolt before heading for his battered truck. He'd vacuumed the glass from the cab, but the broken window and bullet holes in the fender stood out like a warning.

He paused for a moment, glanced back at the house and prayed he wasn't making a big mistake.

Ella had finally fallen asleep, and Bree stepped into the family room to watch a movie with her mother and Deputy Broom. She really needed the distraction. Clint had been gone all day, and she was worried for his safety. Sure, he'd texted her with regular updates, and she appreciated knowing he was okay—for that moment anyway—but he and Shawn were out ruffling feathers and anything could happen. Even another shooting ambush.

And she just plain missed him. Once this was all over, how in the world was she going to adjust to being without him again?

She sighed, garnering her mother's attention. She forced out a smile and thought about her mother's earlier advice to let go of her worry. But how, by trusting God? Sure, that sounded easy, but Clint put his life on the line way too often for Bree to find that peace her mother mentioned.

Bree stifled another sigh and swung her focus back to

the movie. An hour passed, and her anxiety hadn't eased. She couldn't sit any longer. "I'm going to check on Ella."

She headed down the hallway and slipped inside the room. She closed the door behind her and leaned back to take a cleansing breath. Her gaze went to the heavy drapes she'd closed earlier. Now open, they fluttered in the breeze.

Wait, what? They had the air-conditioning running so she knew the window was closed. Clint even checked to be sure it was locked while they waited for Deputy Broom to arrive.

Her heart dropped, and she raced to the crib.

Ella was gone.

No! Oh, no.

A note lay on the mattress. Bree grabbed it.

*I have Ella. Come to the barn alone. Tell anyone and I'll kill the baby.*

All strength left Bree's legs, and she dropped to the floor. Panic flooded in and instinct had her reaching for her phone to call Clint. She patted her pocket. Empty. She'd left it in the living room.

So what? Even if she had it, she couldn't call anyone without risking Ella's life. She had to obey the note. For Ella's sake.

Bree climbed to her feet and held on to the bed post for support. She glanced around the room to locate a weapon of any sort to take with her but she found nothing. Just as well. The killer would probably take it from her anyway.

The killer. A killer waited for her.

She gulped in air and blew it out. Walked to the open window. Swung a leg over the sill.

She paused for a moment to lift her eyes to the sky peppered with stars.

*Father, please help me do the right thing to save Ella.*

* * *

Clint and Shawn had wasted the entire afternoon and early evening waiting for Kier to return to the docks, but as soon as he'd caught sight of Clint, he'd headed back out on the lake.

Fine. If Kier wanted it that way, Clint would figure out another way to talk to him. He marched down the dock, Shawn hurrying to keep up. Near the office, Clint spotted the young woman who'd told them about Jason's argument. Clint rushed toward her as she pulled things out of a locker and put them in a box. He stepped up to her. She held up a hand before he could speak.

"No need to ask," she said. "I'll tell you. Jason argued with Isaac Ellison."

*Isaac.* So they'd been right.

She crossed her arms. "The jerk got me fired. Since the police got a warrant for his boat, and since I was seen talking to you, he claims I told them about the fight." She shook her head. "I was so careful not to say anything, and I still got fired. Unbelievable. Totally unbelievable."

"I'll make sure Dennis Green knows you had nothing to do with getting that warrant," Clint said.

"Ellison is the one you have to convince. He's a big shot around here. As long as he's mad, I won't be getting my job back."

"Then I'll make sure he calls Green."

"Thank you," she said and turned back to cleaning out her locker.

Eager to confront Isaac, Clint jogged down the dock to his truck. Clint revved the engine and Shawn dug out his phone.

"This late in the day we're better off going to Isaac's house," Shawn said. "I'll put his address in my GPS."

Clint followed the GPS directions and was pulling into

Isaac's driveway when Shawn's phone rang. Clint killed the engine and waited for Shawn to finish his call.

He soon shoved the phone into his pocket. "The paint doesn't match Isaac's boat and his wet suits are intact and not of the same brand as the fabric collected."

"I don't care what the forensics say," Clint said. "Isaac is still our best suspect."

Shawn's eyes narrowed. "Forensics don't lie."

"Isaac could have gotten rid of the wet suit and repainted his boat."

"True."

"And if he isn't our guy, then why did he burn those documents right after Bree and I questioned him? And what about the argument with Jason? We can't discount that. We still need to talk to him." Clint grabbed his door handle and was out of the truck in a flash.

He strode up the driveway without waiting for Shawn, but heard him jogging to catch up. Clint's phone rang, and he saw Pete's icon on the screen. Now wasn't the time to talk ranch business.

Clint let the call go to voice mail and pressed his finger on the doorbell, holding it down until Isaac opened the door. Clint pushed past the man and into the living room so fast Isaac couldn't possibly stop him.

"What were you burning on your boat?" Clint asked. "And before you say it's none of my business, I've made it my business, and I'm not leaving here until you answer me."

Isaac crossed his arms. "Then I'll call the police."

"Go ahead," Shawn said as he came to stand by Clint. "Now that the forensic reports for the boats are back, law enforcement will be on your doorstep in no time."

Clint appreciated Shawn's bluff, but Isaac glared at

them. "I didn't do anything wrong so the forensics can't prove I did."

"Are you sure of that?" Shawn asked.

Isaac's eyes narrowed, but he didn't respond.

"We all know you argued with Jason, and we read your last email to him. Couple that with the forensics and…" Clint let his words fall off to imply a connection that hadn't been made.

"Fine," Isaac snapped. "I've been on Jason's boat so I suppose you could have found something that ties to me, but I didn't kill him. We just argued."

Clint wanted to raise a fist in victory, but he held back. "Tell us about the argument."

Isaac scowled. "Jason questioned my decision when I denied benefits for an experimental treatment. I was burning original documents for that case when you caught me."

"Why burn them?" Clint asked.

Isaac hesitated, but Clint glared at him until his shoulders sagged. "I forged Jason's signature on the claim. With you poking around, I was afraid it would come out."

*Interesting.* "Why did you forge his signature?"

"The treatment was within our guidelines and I could have allowed it." Isaac clamped a hand on the back of his neck. "But I was up for a promotion and wanted to make myself look good by keeping our claim costs low. The treatment was expensive so if I approved it, I would have lost out on the promotion."

"You put your career over this person's life?" Clint asked.

"That wasn't the plan. Once I got my promotion, I planned to reverse the denial, but the woman died before I could."

"And Jason discovered what you did," Shawn said.

Isaac nodded. "Abe Geary, the woman's husband, called Jason to complain. I assigned a special code to the denial so if the insured called for any reason, Jason would see the code and forward the call to me. But no. Jason had to be a bleeding heart like always and talked to the man himself, getting all the details and then promising to investigate. That's when Jason found the forged document. He threatened to expose me if I didn't come clean."

Isaac started pacing. "He gave me the weekend to fix it, but he died that same night so I decided I could leave the denial in Jason's name and move on. When you showed up, I knew I had to burn the evidence."

"Seems like a good motive for murder," Clint said.

Isaac blanched. "I may have falsified a claim, but I'm no killer. You need to find the right guy so I don't get jammed up for murder." His eyes lit up. "Hey, what about the husband, Geary? He threatened to kill Jason—in front of witnesses! He marched into the office and went all Rambo on Jason. He's a former marine, I think. Scared us all."

*Marine?* The .338 Lapua was initially designed for the Marines.

"And of course, you didn't tell Geary that you were the one who denied the claim," Shawn said.

"Are you kidding?" Isaac's voice shot up. "Tell a guy who could rip your arms off that you were the guy to blame for what happened to his wife? No way."

Clint glared at Isaac. He was unscrupulous. Beyond caring and unethical. Unfortunately, Clint believed his story was true. He wasn't a killer. They needed to quit wasting time with him and find this crazed soldier before he got to Bree.

# TEN

Bree stood at the end of a very large rifle held by a hulking stranger. His eyes, black as the night, stared down the barrel at her and his index finger rested on the trigger. She held her breath and resisted closing her eyes, knowing the gesture would only reveal her fear.

"You wouldn't let it go, would you?" His deep voice rumbled through the barn lit only by a security light from outside.

She didn't respond as she feared she'd make him angrier.

"You don't know how much I want to pull this trigger. Here, now. Boom. You're toast. But it'd only bring the deputy inside running. Can't have that, so we're going for a little walk and you get to live a few minutes more." His finger drifted away from the trigger.

She released her breath and pulled in another.

He jerked his head toward the back door. "Grab the kid. We're leaving."

She gladly rushed to Ella who was wrapped in her blanket and sleeping in a makeshift crib made of straw bales. The guy had taken care to ensure Ella's safety, and Bree hoped it meant he didn't plan to harm the baby. Bree scooped her into her arms and inhaled her sweet baby scent for comfort.

"Out the back door, now," the guy demanded.

Bree stepped into the night, and he shoved the rifle into her back, pushing her forward. She glanced around, searching for a way out of this mess. She saw Frosty saddled by the door, which struck her as strange. Clint wasn't even home to ride him, so why would the horse be saddled?

For a moment, she imagined jumping on Frosty's back and galloping away, but she couldn't possibly mount the horse and escape with Ella in her arms before the creep shot her and Ella fell to the ground.

Bree continued searching, but the moon slipped under heavy clouds, making it harder for her to see. And sadly, harder for anyone to spot them.

"Take the horse's reins," he demanded.

"Who are you anyway?" She moved closer to Frosty.

"The man who's going to stop you from exposing me," he snapped. "I'm not going away for taking care of a lying, money-grubbing man and his wife."

"You can't be talking about Jason. He was as honest as the day is long."

"Hah! Fat lot you know. He denied my wife's medical treatment just so his crooked insurance company could make more money."

"Jason wouldn't do that. He'd only deny a claim if it was a legitimate denial."

"Tell that to my wife, buried six feet under." He shoved the rifle harder, and Bree nearly stumbled. "Now shut up and keep walking."

She obeyed numbly, knowing that when they got to wherever he was taking her, he'd surely end her life. And then what would happen to Ella? Or Clint? He'd been investigating right alongside her. Once she was out of the way, would he be this man's next target?

* * *

Back in his truck, Clint's phone rang. He glanced at caller ID to see Bree's name. Perfect. He could warn her and the deputy to keep an eye out for Geary.

"It's Bree and Ella." Marie's frantic tone shot through the phone. "I went to check on them. The bedroom window was jimmied and they're missing."

*Geary.* At the thought of the tough soldier abducting Bree and baby Ella, Clint's heart constricted. "I'm on my way. Don't go outside for any reason."

Clint disconnected and updated Shawn. "Use the drive time to find anything you can about Geary. Maybe it'll help us figure out where he's taken them."

"I'm sorry, man. I hate that Bree and the baby are missing." Shawn dug out his phone. "But we'll find them."

"I know that, but will we be in time?" Just saying the words sent acid rising up Clint's throat. He swallowed hard and got them on the highway where he pushed the pedal harder. His ancient truck shuddered from exertion, but he didn't let up, not even when Shawn finished his call.

"Geary's got priors for aggravated assault and deadly conduct."

Clint glanced at Shawn. "I'm not familiar with deadly conduct."

"In Texas, if you engage in any type of conduct that you know, or should know, will place someone else at risk of suffering serious bodily injury, you can be charged with deadly conduct. Geary pulled a weapon on a guy after he sideswiped Geary's truck." Shawn paused for a minute. "And he used a Kivaari semi-auto takedown rifle."

Clint had read about the pricey new rifle that broke down into a backpack-sized package. "Chambered for a .338 Lapua Magnum and a perfect way to bring power to the game and not be seen with a rifle."

"Exactly. It means we're dealing with a guy who knows how to kill. I should request backup at the ranch."

"Not yet," Clint warned. "I want to assess the situation in stealth mode before sending some rookie in to botch the job and make things worse for Bree."

"Good point."

Searching for any lead, Clint ran through everything they'd learned that day. "Pete! I got a call from him when I was going into Isaac's house. I thought it was ranch business but might be something else. Grab my phone and see if he left a message."

Shawn took the phone from the console. "He did."

"Pete hates to leave messages so it's gotta be important." Clint gave Shawn the voice mail password, and he started playing the recording.

"This here's Pete Allgood," Pete said. "Some fool cut the fence on the north side of the property. I fixed it, but on the way back, I found me some ATV tracks that led to a fresh campsite by the ridge. Looks like we might have a squatter."

"Or a killer," Clint mumbled.

"You think Geary's the camper?" Shane stowed Clint's phone.

"Yes," Clint replied, and as a vision of the location flashed before his eyes, his gut cramped hard. "And he might be planning to use the ridge's steep drop off to end Bree's life."

The gunman shoved Bree forward, and she stumbled into a small camp consisting of a tiny tent and fire ring. Maybe this guy wasn't going to kill her after all. Maybe he was going to hold her here for some reason.

"Loop the reins over the branch and put the baby in the tent," he commanded.

Bree hated to leave Ella, but with a rifle to her back she had no choice. She secured Frosty before going to the tent. She kissed Ella's cheek and cuddled her close. "Don't worry, precious. I won't let anything bad happen to you."

She settled Ella on a sleeping bag then backed out and faced the man. "Don't you think I should know your name?"

"Why not. Abe Geary, husband of Alicia, who died because your friend denied her claim."

Bree's gut said something was wrong with his story, but arguing would only increase his burning anger. "I get that you blame Jason, but why kill Laura, too?"

"Was the only way I could take him out and make it look like an accident. Now enough with the questions. Get on the horse."

"The horse? Why?"

"Simple, really. I'll spook him, and he'll take off with you in the saddle. Just to the east is a ridge with a nice drop-off. You'll go over the edge, and unlike a gunshot, even if you scream, you won't alert the deputy back at the ranch house."

He gestured at Frosty. "Mount up."

Bree took slow steps toward the horse. Fear climbed up and threatened to swamp her as she searched for a way out. Her brain was a jumbled mess of thoughts, but a sudden vision of Clint riding in to the save her and Ella overpowered them.

*Father, please, if Mom's right and You sent Clint to protect me, get him here before it's too late.*

Clint galloped through the dark, trusting Trident to safely take him to the squatter's camp. Clint had hoped to bring Shawn along to apprehend Geary, but with Frosty missing Clint had no other horse for Shawn to ride, and they couldn't risk Geary hearing the ATV engine.

As it was, Clint now approached the camp and had to slow to a trot and hope Trident didn't give him away.

Clint raised night vision binoculars and caught sight of Bree climbing up on Frosty. Clint sighed out his relief over seeing Bree still alive. Her arms were empty, though. Where was Ella? Was she safe?

A man—Geary, Clint assumed—pointed his rifle at her. Was Geary planning to scare Frosty into bolting?

Frosty didn't startle easily, but a gunshot would send him running. Clint quickly calculated the ridge was about one hundred yards to the east. Frosty could easily get up steam in that distance and go barreling over the edge.

Clint couldn't let that happen, but how could he stop the guy from firing?

Clint had grabbed a rifle from the house, but he couldn't use it to take out Geary without sending Frosty bolting. Past outings proved Bree was a good rider, but could she handle a spooked horse in the dark? Clint couldn't risk it.

Hoping a solution would present itself, he dismounted and eased forward, leading Trident by the reins.

"What about Ella?" Bree asked the man. "What will happen to her?"

"I'd never hurt a kid," he said. "I'll make sure someone knows she's in the tent and will come for her."

Even at a distance, Clint could hear Bree's heavy sigh in response, and Clint felt the same relief.

"I just don't get it," Bree said. "If you needed money for your wife's medical treatment, why not sell the boat?"

*And the pricey gun,* Clint thought as he dismounted and moved closer.

"Bought it and this baby with Alicia's life insurance money." He patted his gun. "The boat gave me the perfect way to kill that money-grubber. Now that that's done, I'll sell it."

So he *did* kill Jason and Laura. Now he wanted to kill Bree.

Not happening.

Clint signaled Trident to stay put, but left him free in the event that Clint had to call for his assistance.

"How exactly did you kill them?" Bree asked.

"No big deal. Tied my boat up alongside them and let my engine fill their cabin with carbon monoxide."

"But they had a detector."

"Earlier that week, I rewired it so the lights worked but the thing wouldn't go off. Once they were goners, I changed it back and messed with the generator to make it look like an accident."

"But what about gouging Jason's boat? That didn't help make it look like an accident."

"Didn't plan on some dude motoring up in the middle of the night. I had to take off in a hurry, scraping their boat in the process. Figured no one would think anything of it. Then you did."

Clint appreciated getting details of what went down with Jason and Laura, but he appreciated more the time Bree bought, allowing him to move into position behind a tree a few feet from Geary.

Frosty lifted his head, telling Clint he'd picked up his scent. Clint held his breath and hoped Geary didn't notice.

"The police will finally figure this out, you know," Bree said. "And they'll find the damage on your boat as proof."

"Already got it fixed, and as soon as I take care of you, I'm selling the thing."

Clint couldn't believe that with a gun fixed on her, Bree had the presence of mind to keep asking questions.

"So tell me," she said. "Did killing Jason make you feel better? Lessen your grief?"

Geary went still for a long moment. "Not rightly sure, yet." He dropped Frosty's reins. "But I *do* know that I'm not going to prison."

"So you're going to kill another innocent person?"

"Looks like it." He took Frosty's bridle and pointed him at the ridge.

Clint needed to act.

He shot out from behind the tree and grabbed for Geary's rifle. Geary jerked to the side. Clint tried to get a grip on the gun to wrench it from Geary's hands. The rifle exploded with a deafening report then hit the ground.

Frosty bolted.

"No!" Clint shouted and spun to go back for Trident.

Clint made it only a few feet before Geary tackled him from behind, leaving Bree racing toward what seemed like certain death.

Frosty tore through the black of night and panic assailed Bree. She flattened her body over Frosty's head and reached for the reins.

The leather slapped her fingers but she couldn't catch hold. Clint. She needed Clint. He'd likely arrived on Trident. Could he get free of Geary and catch up to Frosty?

Another shot rang through the night.

*No. No.* Had Geary killed Clint?

Her heart creased, but Frosty suddenly veered left and thoughts of Clint evaporated as she tried to hang on. She'd learned how to handle a bolting horse, but fear twisted her thoughts into a tangled web.

*Think. Think. Think.*

*Sit back up.* Yes. Sitting up would keep her from flying over Frosty's shoulders if he made a sharper turn, or over his neck if he dropped his head. She slowly rose up, the wind hitting her full on and unsettling her more.

She had to let go of her fear. Her worry. Trust God to keep her safe and relax so she could get back into Frosty's rhythm and not add to his anxiety.

*Oh, God, please. Help me. Help Clint.*

She heard hooves pounding behind her. Geary didn't have a horse. It had to be Clint on Trident, as the horse only let Clint ride him. The hooves sounded closer. Gaining on them.

A loud whistle came from behind. Clint was trying to call Frosty, but her horse didn't lose a beat and they continued racing toward the ridge. If Clint didn't succeed in turning Frosty soon, she'd have to take her chances at bailing. But poor Frosty would still go over the edge.

Clint whistled again. She felt Frosty falter for a moment. Just a second really, but it was a good sign.

Clint whistled a third time. Frosty slowed a touch, allowing the more powerful Trident to catch up and come alongside them.

"I'm going to grab Frosty's reins," Clint shouted.

He leaned to the side. A dangerous and risky move. She hoped Clint's high school rodeo experience kept him safe.

Trident surged, and Clint snagged a rein.

He swung back up in the saddle and changed Trident's direction. Frosty followed.

*Thank You, God!*

They continued to gallop, and she kept her attention on not falling off as Clint directed both horses to turn and gradually brought them to a stop.

Clint dropped from his horse, grabbed Bree from the saddle and wrapped his powerful arms around her. "If I... If you... I couldn't lose you. I just couldn't."

She clung to him, but he suddenly pushed her away and moved them into a copse of trees.

"I managed to knock Geary senseless long enough to get on Trident and come after you without taking a bullet in the back," he said.

"But he still has the rifle."

"I had no time to go after the gun. I had to stop Frosty before he reached the ridge. Now I need you to stay behind a tree while I take care of Geary." Clint grabbed his rifle from Trident's saddle and headed toward camp on foot.

Bree knew she should obey his instructions, but she couldn't sit back and do nothing. Especially when Ella was still alone in the tent. Bree moved silently toward the campsite. She stopped behind a tree and peeked around. Geary stood with Ella in his arms, and Clint held his rifle on them. Geary's gun was nowhere in sight.

Bree had to hold on to the tree to keep herself from racing to save Ella.

"You hear the ATVs closing in on us?" Clint asked. "That'll be the deputies I called on my way back here. You have no way out."

Geary looked at Ella then back at Clint. "Fine. You win."

"Lay the baby on the ground and step back."

Geary's shoulders slumped, and he followed Clint's directions. Ella started whimpering. Clint moved to Ella and scooped her up with his free hand.

"I'm here, honey. It's okay," he said, but his focus never left Geary,

Bree wanted to run to Ella, but she couldn't risk distracting Clint and give Geary the upper hand again. So she hung back, her heart filled with love for Clint.

Shawn arrived and soon had Geary in handcuffs. Clint

set down his rifle and lifted Ella to his chest, his face filled with emotions.

Bree stood in amazement. He'd come to care for Ella. Really care for her. Dare she hope they could find a way to be together as a family?

"Feels good to exchange my rifle for you," he whispered. "A perfect trade. Too bad it can't be permanent."

Bree's heart shattered.

Nothing had changed.

Clint was going back to the SEALs, and she could do nothing to stop him.

# ELEVEN

At daybreak, Clint burned off his unease from the previous night by galloping across his land on Trident. The powerful stallion's breath came in loud puffs as his feet pummeled the ground. They charged down a winding access road then over wide-open pastures.

Man, Clint loved this place. Every inch of it. It had been his favorite spot on earth until he'd come to live here under his granddad's severe reign. Then he'd only wanted to run far away from it.

Now, he desperately wanted to stay. To be with Bree. To raise little Ella. To see them both smiling and happy. To lavish love on them and receive it in return. The love he'd missed since his parents died.

*Wait.*

He pulled on Trident's reins, drawing him to a stop. Clint jumped down and patted the horse's neck. "I've been convincing myself I couldn't be here because of my calling, but that wasn't it, was it, fella? I couldn't risk losing Bree like I lost my parents. Comes down to trusting God, I suppose. If it meant I could be with Bree, I could do that, right? Yeah, I could. For her. But I'd still need a job to support her and Ella."

He heard hooves pounding toward him, and he spun to

see Shawn racing across the range. Clint's heart jumped into his throat. Had something bad happened to Bree?

He fought the urge to climb back on Trident and charge toward Shawn, but stood not so patiently waiting for him to arrive.

"Everything okay?" he asked.

"Okay? No, man! You're standing here talking to your horse when the woman you love is packing up to leave."

Which was why Clint had taken off. "Even if I wanted to stay here and be with her, what kind of job can I get around here that will pay enough to support a wife and child? I have a good bit socked away in savings, but that won't work long-term and a high school diploma just doesn't cut it."

Shawn kicked his leg over the saddle and dropped to the ground. "Therapy horses."

"Say what?"

"You have all this land, expertise in horses, and you just said you have money in savings. It shouldn't cost too much to add to your stock and set up facilities. You've seen guys struggling with PTSD. They need help, man. You can provide it through a therapy horse program."

"Therapy horses, huh?" Clint mulled the idea over. "Helping vets. I like the sound of that."

"And you'd never have to leave the ranch if you didn't want to." Shawn grinned. "Bree would love that."

A picture of Bree and Ella on the ranch formed in his mind. Ella on a pony, other children, too. Theirs. He couldn't find any reason not to do this. Well, maybe he had to ask God for His opinion, but Clint had such peace about the idea he knew God would be okay with it, too.

"Thanks, man." Clint climbed onto Trident's back. "You're welcome to ride back with me, but then make yourself scarce."

Shawn laughed. "You just go get her. I'll take the back way home."

"I will and that's a promise."

Bree loaded the portable crib into her scarred vehicle. She'd forgotten all about the bullet holes. And the home she was returning to was in even worse shape. She was leaving this amazing place behind, leaving Clint behind, and heading back to reality.

She'd be raising Ella alone. Not what she'd wanted. Not when she'd seen how good Clint was with Ella. And there'd be no other guy for Bree. At least, not for the foreseeable future. It was going to take even longer to get over Clint this time. Being thrown together like they'd been the last few days showed her how wonderful it would be to have him around full-time. Now she wanted that and nothing less.

Hooves thundered in the distance and dust filtered into the air. Had to be Shawn or Clint or both of them returning from their rides. She had no idea what Shawn had wanted, but after they'd talked for a bit, he'd been almost frantic to find Clint.

She went back inside to retrieve Ella's car seat and haul it out to the car. The hooves pounded closer. Hopefully it was Clint so she could say goodbye, but she wouldn't look up to be disappointed if it was only Shawn. She clicked the last strap in place and heard the horse stop shy of her car.

"You can't go."

It was Clint's voice, and her heart soared as she backed out of the car. Her gaze went to his, and her whole body filled with longing to have him as part of her family.

"I have a plan to leave the military and stay here," he said. "It'll mean living lean and mean for a while, but I think we can do it."

"Tell me about it," she said, not willing to let herself get excited until she knew more.

"Let's sit down." He led her to the porch where an old swing hung from wooden rafters.

They sat and Clint stared ahead. "I used to sit out here at sunset with my parents. The skies were filled with color and God's promises, but I quit believing in them when my parents died. Now I think God's given me the answer to our problem." Clint swiveled to face her and took her hands. "Shawn suggested I use the ranch for horse therapy for vets suffering from PTSD."

"What an amazing idea." Her heart soared then fell as she thought about it. "But even if it would be great for the vets, is it right for you? Are you okay with leaving the SEALs and being landlocked again? Living a boring old life on a small ranch."

"If you'll agree to marry me, I can live anywhere."

*Marriage.* He wanted to marry her.

"Marry you? Isn't that awful sudden?"

"Is it? I love you, Bree. That's no secret, right?"

"Right," she replied, her mind awash with thoughts, but she couldn't focus with his gaze fixed on her like that.

"And I get the feeling you love me, too," he said.

"I do." She smiled at him. "So much, but—"

"But what? We're in love. We have a way to be together, and I want to be a father to Ella. The kind of father my dad was before he died. Please say you'll marry me, and we can work out all the rest."

"Yes." She flung her arms around his neck. "Yes! Yes! Yes!"

He drew back and suddenly his lips were on hers, the love nearly bursting her heart reflected in his kiss.

Bree heard the porch door squeak open.

"Everything okay out here?" her mother asked.

Bree pulled free to look at her mother who held a drooling Ella. Bree got up to take Ella, but before she could, Clint had the precious child in his arms.

"We're going to be a family," he said to Ella while slipping his arm around Bree and drawing her tightly to his side. "I don't suppose it's too early to start looking for Ella's first pony."

Bree smiled up at Clint making sure she transmitted her love for him.

"Things are more than okay," she said to her mom without taking her gaze from Clint. "They're absolutely perfect."

* * * * *

*If you liked this story, pick up these other stories from Susan Sleeman:*

*SILENT NIGHT STANDOFF*
*EXPLOSIVE ALLIANCE*
*HIGH-CALIBER HOLIDAY*
*EMERGENCY RESPONSE*
*SILENT SABOTAGE*
*CHRISTMAS CONSPIRACY*

*Available now from Love Inspired Suspense!*

*Find more great reads at www.LoveInspired.com.*

Dear Reader,

Helping others through military service is such a noble profession. I respect and am in awe of this service to our country, often given at great personal sacrifice. So, I wanted to take a moment to thank the brave men and women serving in our armed forces.

We are all free to live. Free to express our faith publicly. Free to be who we are in this great country we live in, and for that we owe a great debt of gratitude to these men and women. So join with me in praying not only for our military personnel, but for their families who give so much so that their loved ones can protect us and our freedoms.

May God bless each and every person from the freshly enlisted private to the wise armed forces leaders. We are truly blessed because of your and your families' sacrifices!

If you'd like to learn more about my other books, please stop by my website at www.susansleeman.com. I also love hearing from readers so please contact me via email, susan@susansleeman.com, on my Facebook page, www.facebook.com/SusanSleemanBooks, or write to me c/o Love Inspired, HarperCollins 24th floor, 195 Broadway, New York, NY 10007.

*Susan Sleeman*

# Get 2 Free Books,
## Plus 2 Free Gifts—
### just for trying the Reader Service!

**YES!** Please send me 2 FREE Love Inspired® Suspense novels and my 2 FREE mystery gifts (gifts are worth about $10 retail). After receiving them, if I don't wish to receive any more books, I can return the shipping statement marked "cancel." If I don't cancel, I will receive 4 brand-new novels every month and be billed just $5.24 each for the regular-print edition or $5.74 each for the larger-print edition in the U.S., or $5.74 each for the regular-print edition or $6.24 each for the larger-print edition in Canada. That's a savings of at least 13% off the cover price. It's quite a bargain! Shipping and handling is just 50¢ per book in the U.S. and 75¢ per book in Canada.* I understand that accepting the 2 free books and gifts places me under no obligation to buy anything. I can always return a shipment and cancel at any time. Even if I never buy another book, the 2 free books and gifts are mine to keep forever.

Please check one: ☐ Love Inspired Suspense Regular-Print ☐ Love Inspired Suspense Larger-Print
(153/353 IDN GLQE)   (107/307 IDN GLQF)

Name _____ (PLEASE PRINT) _____

Address _____ Apt. #

City _____ State/Prov. _____ Zip/Postal Code

Signature (if under 18, a parent or guardian must sign)

### Mail to the Reader Service:
**IN U.S.A.:** P.O. Box 1867, Buffalo, NY 14240-1867
**IN CANADA:** P.O. Box 611, Fort Erie, Ontario L2A 9Z9

**Want to try two free books from another series?**
**Call 1-800-873-8635 or visit www.ReaderService.com.**

* Terms and prices subject to change without notice. Prices do not include applicable taxes. Sales tax applicable in N.Y. Canadian residents will be charged applicable taxes. Offer not valid in Quebec. This offer is limited to one order per household. Books received may not be as shown. Not valid for current subscribers to Love Inspired Suspense books. All orders subject to credit approval. Credit or debit balances in a customer's account(s) may be offset by any other outstanding balance owed by or to the customer. Please allow 4 to 6 weeks for delivery. Offer available while quantities last.

**Your Privacy**—The Reader Service is committed to protecting your privacy. Our Privacy Policy is available online at www.ReaderService.com or upon request from the Reader Service.

We make a portion of our mailing list available to reputable third parties that offer products we believe may interest you. If you prefer that we not exchange your name with third parties, or if you wish to clarify or modify your communication preferences, please visit us at www.ReaderService.com/consumerschoice or write to us at Reader Service Preference Service, P.O. Box 9062, Buffalo, NY 14240-9062. Include your complete name and address.

LIS17R

SPECIAL EXCERPT FROM

Love Inspired.
SUSPENSE

*When one of their own goes missing, an elite FBI K-9
unit will stop at nothing to bring him back.*

*Read on for a sneak preview of
GUARDIAN,
the first book in the exciting new series*
**Classified K-9 Unit.**

The daylight broke over the horizon of the industrial
district, and muted morning light slashed through the high
windows of the large two-floor warehouse. FBI agent Leo
Gallagher pressed his back to the wall inside the cavernous
structure's entrance. The air was cool but heavy with a mix
of anticipation and caution.

His heart rate increased. Not much, but enough that he
took a calming breath. He tightened his hold on the leash
of his canine partner, a chocolate Labrador named True.

The open floor plan of the bottom level was filled with
containers and pallets that provided too many hiding
places. That could be a problem. Shadows lurked above
and in the recesses of the corners.

Almost time? Leo glanced at fellow FBI agent Jake
Morrow and his canine, a Belgian Malinois named Buddy.

Behind his tactical face guard, Jake nodded and signaled
for Leo and True to proceed into the murky depths of the
purported hideout of the notorious Dupree syndicate. The
criminal organization that the elite FBI K-9 unit had been
working around the clock to bring down for months.

LISEXP0317

But every time the team got close, the crime boss, Reginald Dupree, and his second in command, his uncle Angus Dupree, managed to escape.

Not going to happen this time. The first time could have been coincidence, but after the second and third times, something else was going on. That was why Leo's boss had been tight-lipped about this raid. No one outside the tight circle of the team knew of today's operation in case there was a leak.

True's ears perked up. The scruff of his neck rose. He emitted a deep growl from his throat.

Breath stalling, Leo paused, scanning the area for whatever threat his partner sensed.

Four men with automatic weapons appeared from around the sides of the two containers. A barrage of gunfire erupted. The deafening noise bounced off the walls.

Leo's heart revved into overdrive. His pulse pounded in his ears as he dropped to one knee to return fire.

"Down!" Leo shouted to True.

*Don't miss*
*GUARDIAN by Terri Reed,*
*available wherever*
*Love Inspired® Suspense ebooks are sold.*

www.LoveInspired.com

LISEXP0317

*Returning to her Amish community, Lizbeth Mullet comes
face-to-face with her teenage crush, Fredrik Lapp. As he
builds a bond with her son and she falls for him all over
again, will revealing the secret she holds turn out to be their
undoing—or the key to their happily-ever-after?*

Read on for a sneak preview of
HER SECRET AMISH CHILD by Cheryl Williford,
*available April 2017 from Love Inspired!*

"Lie still. You may have broken something," Lizbeth
instructed.

His hand moved and then his arm. Blue eyes—so like
her son's—opened to slits. He blinked at her. A shaggy brow
arched in question. Full, well-shaped lips moved, but no
words came out.

She leaned back in surprise. The man on the ground was
Fredrik Lapp, her brother's childhood friend. The last man in
Pinecraft she wanted to see. "Are you all right?" she asked,
bending close.

His coloring looked normal enough, but she knew nothing
about broken bones or head trauma. She looked down the
length of his body. His clothes were dirty but seemed intact.

The last time she'd seen him, she'd been a skinny girl of
nineteen, and he'd been a wiry young man of twenty-three.
Now he was a fully matured man. One who could rip her life
apart if he learned about the secret she'd kept all these years.

He coughed several times and scowled as he drew in a

deep breath.

"Is the *kinner* all right?" Fredrik's voice sounded deeper and raspier than it had years ago. With a grunt, he braced himself with his arms and struggled into a sitting position.

Lizbeth glanced Benuel's way. He was looking at them, his young face pinched with concern. Her heart ached for the intense, worried child.

"*Ya*, he's fine," she assured Fredrik and tried to hold him down as he started to move about. "Please don't get up. Let me get some help first. You might have really hurt yourself."

He ignored her direction and rose to his feet, dusting off the long legs of his dark trousers. "I got the wind knocked out of me, that's all."

He peered at his bleeding arm, shrugged his broad shoulders and rotated his neck as she'd seen him do a hundred times as a boy.

"That was a foolish thing you did," he muttered, his brow arched.

"What was?" she asked, mesmerized by the way his muscles bulged along his freckled arm. It had to be wonderful to be strong and afraid of nothing.

He gestured toward the boy. "Letting your *soh* run wild like that? He could have been killed. Why didn't you hold his hand while you crossed the road?"

*Don't miss*
*HER SECRET AMISH CHILD by Cheryl Williford,*
*available April 2017 wherever*
*Love Inspired® books and ebooks are sold.*

www.LoveInspired.com